STUMBLING INTO THE HOLIDAYS

STUMBLING THROUGH LIFE BOOK THREE

MOLLY O'HARE

COPYRIGHT

Molly O'Hare
First Print: December 2020
ISBN-13: 978-1-7328338-5-2
Be You Publishing, LLC
www.MollyOHareauthor.com

DEDICATION

This book is dedicated to you. You're what matters in this world and never forget that. Anyone that tries to tell you differently, mentally punch them in the face. They don't deserve you.
Keep being a Unicorn.
You're what makes this world a better place.
I promise.
Love you always,
Molly

CHAPTER ONE

"HOLLY RICHMAN, do *not* make me call the fire department again. Put down that spatula. *Now!*" Ben crossed his arms over his chest as he glared down at his wife. "You made those poor firefighters leave their Thanksgiving meal 'cause you *wanted to baste the turkey.*"

The corner of Ben's mouth turned up as an amused twinkle appeared in his eyes. "Who knew flames could shoot out of an oven that far?"

Seriously, though, there were a good few seconds Ben thought their house was going to catch fire or at least their kitchen.

However, the moment the words left Ben's mouth, Holly's jaw dropped. "You said you weren't gonna bring that up again. You *promised!*" She narrowed her eyes on her betraying husband. "How could you?"

He cocked his brow as he pointed to the scorch marks on the wall. "No. I *said* when the marks fade or get painted over, only *then* I wouldn't bring it up." He walked to the scorch marks before smirking her way. "And there is no way in hell I'm ever letting you paint over them."

"You jerk."

At Holly's angry growl, Ben tried to hold it together. There was nothing better than riling Holly up first thing in the morning. To him, it was always a damn good day when he could get under her skin. Maybe that's why it was one of his favorite activities.

What could he say? An annoyed Holly was *always* a fun Holly.

However, before Holly could retort, he grabbed her shoulders, dragging her and the scowling expression of one Holly Richman into his arms. At her annoyed grunt, Ben laughed as he brought his lips down to hers. "Love you, Grace."

"Screw you."

As he ignored her annoyance, Ben leaned in lightly brushing his lips to her ear. "It'll be my pleasure. I think Jimmy has Helen in the back room. Wanna see if we can do a quickie?"

When Ben heard Holly's breath hitch, he smirked before nibbling on her earlobe.

Well, this morning just got a hell of a lot more interesting.

Sadly, for him, though, Ben's win was short-lived. Instead of doing what he wanted to do, which was to lift Holly onto the counter and have himself his own Thanksgiving feast, Holly lifted her foot before stomping on his. *Hard.*

"Oww! What the hell, Grace?"

"I don't think so." Holly pulled away and crossed her arms over her ample chest. "You don't get to make fun of me then go to pound town on my lady bits," she whisper-shouted at him.

"Pound town?" Ben arched his brow.

"Yes. Pound town. What else do you want me to call it?" Holly's lips thinned as she glared daggers at him. "I should sic Waffles on you."

With her threat, both of Ben's brows lifted in surprise. "Oh, really?"

Instantly, that famous twitch Holly got in her left eye when she was annoyed appeared. Was it wrong of him to want to laugh? Probably, but did that stop him? Hell no.

"Fine. Jimmy then."

Ben recrossed his arms over his chest as he cocked his head to the side, eyeing her like she was crazy.

"Okay. Whatever. My dad."

When he didn't move, Holly threw her hands in the air. "Fine, you jerkface. I'll do it myself."

Ready for Holly's tantrum, Ben had his arms open before the words were out of her mouth. As he caught her with ease, he held her against his body, molding her curves to his front. "You know, Grace, if you'd put this much effort into your cooking as you do trying to get me, you probably *wouldn't attempt to* burn the house down as much."

"You assho—"

"Mom!"

Perfect timing.

As their son Jimmy walked into the kitchen carrying his little sister Helen in his arms, the corner of Ben's mouth turned up. As carefully as he could, he gently placed Holly back down so she wouldn't topple over. He knew if he didn't make sure her feet were on the floor, her ass would have been there instead.

It might be fun to mess with Holly, but seeing her fall over wasn't in his plans today.

Holly shot Ben a dirty look telling him this was far from over before she shifted to their kids. However, the moment Holly turned with a little *too* much force, she almost slammed her hip into their kitchen island.

It took everything inside of Ben to not burst out laughing when he saw Holly shoot the island the same glare she'd given him only moments ago.

"Mom?"

With one last death stare at the island, she turned to Jimmy. "Yeah, baby?" As she reached out to take Helen, she sent Ben another glare for good measure.

"What?" Ben smirked, crossing his arms over his chest.

"I've got her." Jimmy maneuvered so Holly couldn't take the little girl. "I changed her diaper but I think she's hungry. She's still really fussy. Even Ripley can't calm her down."

Ben's heart warmed as he watched Jimmy hold his baby sister close to his chest. From the moment they'd brought Peanut home from the hospital, Jimmy wanted to be fully involved. He took his big brother role very seriously. At first, he wasn't as excited about changing diapers, but he insisted on doing it anyway.

Jimmy had come so far since the night of the break-in at the clinic.

Even though Helen was only seven and a half months old, Jimmy was already extremely protective of her.

As Ben leaned back onto the counter, he watched a look of horror appear on Jimmy's face as he saw what Holly was still holding in her hand.

"Mom, why do you have a spatula?" Jimmy's huge eyes widened as he turned to Ben. "Dad, is she cooking again? Please tell me she's not trying to cook. I thought we talked about this? Grandpa Henry was here and everything."

Ben pointed to the scorch marks on the wall with a smirk. "I think she wants to go for round two."

Holly gasped. "Both of you can kiss my butt!" She glared at her betraying family before she plucked the baby from Jimmy's hands. "At least I have you, Peanut. You wouldn't make fun of your Momma, would you?"

Although the moment Holly had Helen positioned in her arms, the baby looked over her shoulder and right to her father. Instantly, Helen's eyes sparkled as she reached out her little arms trying to get Ben's attention.

"Not you too!" Holly's lips thinned as the little girl made a cooing noise to Ben making her desire clear.

Damn, I love my family. Ben pushed himself off the counter before gently grabbing Helen from his wife's arms. "She's a smart girl, Grace. What do you expect?"

"All of you are jerks." Holly stomped over to the fridge to grab a bottle of milk she'd placed there earlier in the morning. "I get zero respect here."

To no one's surprise, the moment the fridge door cracked open, Waffles, Ripley, and Twitch all came running into the kitchen.

"Oh, come on!"

Waffles, ever the one in charge of their gang, took a small step in front of the others. He then pushed himself onto his back legs, making him look like a meerkat, a trick Holly taught him years ago. Ripley instantly followed suit, with Twitch trying his best to do the same all while his little head bobbed from side-to-side.

"Are you freaking kidding me? When I open the fridge that does *not* mean you automatically get something." Holly narrowed her eyes at Waffles who dangled his tongue out of the right side of his mouth.

"No, it's much worse." Jimmy ran over to Waffles

scratching him behind the ears. "Mom's trying to cook. *Again*."

Within seconds, all three animals dropped to the floor and quickly hightailed it over to Ben's legs to hide behind him. Holly's eyes immediately followed the traitors as she glared daggers at their four-legged fur babies. "How could you?"

Waffles, the jerk himself, trotted in front of Ben before he plopped his happy Corgi butt on the floor giving Holly a side-eye to end all side-eyes.

"Put that attitude away, Waffles, or you'll never get another treat again."

Great, now there is gonna be another standoff.

Ben put twenty bucks on Waffles in this sparring match. He'd been on the other end of Waffles' judgmental looks too many times and already knew how this was going to end.

On second thought, maybe he should make that forty bucks instead?

A smug expression appeared on Waffles' face as his eyes moved to Jimmy who already had his hand in the treat jar.

Immediately, Holly spun toward her son. "Don't you dare, mister."

Jimmy ignored her with a shrug as he quickly tossed each dog a treat before giving a small cat treat to Twitch. When he looked back at his mom, the corners of his mouth turned into a smile. "What? They all did a trick. You always say we should reward good behavior."

This kid is good! It was like he was made for our family. Who knew messing with Holly would end up being a family tradition? I can't wait to tell Henry about this.

Holly's brows shot to the ceiling in shock at Jimmy's audacity. "And you think *this* is good behavior?" She waved her hands through the air pointing at Waffles.

A playful smile appeared on Jimmy's face as he answered her, "They distracted you enough to put down the spatula, didn't they? I think that deserves two treats." With that, Jimmy tossed them all another one.

"That's my son!" Ben held out his hand to Jimmy who cheerfully high-fived him.

"I'm gonna remember this."

"I'm sure you will." Ben strolled over to his wife, gently moving Helen out of the way before kissing the top of Holly's head.

"If you weren't holding Peanut, I'd stomp on your foot again." Holly sent him another dirty look.

"Good thing I'm holding her then, huh?"

"You just wait. I'm gonna get you."

"Mom, violence is bad. You shouldn't threaten people. We've talked about this before. Unless it's Grandpa Henry, he said *he's* allowed to threaten anyone."

Holly crossed her arms over her chest as she watched him. "Did he now?"

"Yeah. He said since he's the oldest he's allowed to do whatever he wants. Just like Mrs. Mildred."

"Sounds about right." Ben snorted before grabbing the bottle from Holly's hand.

"Mom, you really shouldn't threaten people. It's not nice."

Holly's eyes snapped to Ben as she sent him a death glare.

"Don't look at me like that, the kid's right. Threatening people is bad." Ben held back his laugh. There was nothing better than getting schooled by a child. Especially, when it was Jimmy schooling Holly and not him. Lord knows that'd happened too many times for him to count.

The kid was smart.

Just as Holly's eye began to twitch again, Jimmy barked out a laugh. "Geez, Mom you sure are fun to mess with. Now, I know why Dad likes to call Officer Jones up every once in a while."

Holly's reply was a flat smile as her eyes hardened on her husband. "You really need to stop doing that."

"At this point, my goal is to actually have him arrest you." Ben winked which made Holly's jaw firm in irritation. "I'm glad I'm here for your entertainment."

"Me too." Jimmy sent her a toothy smile.

"I second that," Ben's voice dropped an octave as he eyed her up and down.

However, the moment Holly opened her mouth to reply, his highness barked which caused her to snap her attention to her dog. "You better not be agreeing with them too, Waffles."

The Corgi barked again before turning to Ripley who replied with her own bark.

Holly threw her hands in the air. "You've got to be kidding me."

Okay, time to step in. She's seconds from really losing it.

Ben grabbed Holly's hand dragging her toward him and the baby. Quickly he gave her a chaste kiss on the lips. "We're only messing with you, Grace."

"Yeah, Mom. We love you." Jimmy ran to them giving them both a hug.

"I don't believe you," Holly remarked, as she relaxed in Ben's arms for a split second.

"That's 'cause you keep tryin' to cook." Jimmy laughed as he jumped back giving Holly a playful smile.

"Oh, for the love of all things," Holly groaned, rolling her eyes.

"Come on, guys, let's go before Mom's head explodes."

Jimmy ran out of the kitchen laughing as an all too eager pack of animals scurried after him.

Once they were out of the room, Holly turned to her husband. "You taught him how to gang up on me." Holly angrily snapped her arms over her chest staring him down.

"Nah, wasn't me." He shook his head. "That was all Lord Waffles." The corners of Ben's mouth turned up as he pushed their daughter higher onto his shoulder.

"Lord Waffles doesn't call Officer Jones."

"He would if he could."

Holly gaped at Ben for a few moments before completely giving up. As she flicked her eyes to the ceiling, a heavy sigh escaped her. "You're probably right. All of you are jerks and he's the ringleader."

"That he is, now come here and let me kiss you."

"No." She took a step away from him. However, the moment Holly tripped over thin air, she caught herself on the counter shooting him another death glare. "Don't you say a word."

Ben let out a laugh as he winked her way. "Grace why would I say anything about you tripping over nothing?"

"Don't you wink at me. It's your fault I tripped anyway."

"That so?"

"Yeah."

Ben quickly advanced on Holly, making sure to keep Peanut softly at his side. "How's it my fault you tripped?"

"It's always your fault. One moment I'm standing and the next I'm on the floor."

"I wasn't even home the last time that happened."

"Yeah, but Jimmy told you about it so that makes it your fault."

"Sure, whatever, it can be my fault you stumble around

like a newborn giraffe attempting to walk for the first time."
He leaned in trying to kiss her but Holly darted away from
his advance.

"Hey!"

Ben's brows arched. "Am I wrong?"

"No, but you don't need to compare me to a baby
giraffe. I've got more grace than that."

Ben nodded. "Okay, sure, you do." After taking another
step in her direction, he had Holly in his arms. "Love you,
baby."

Even though she protested, instantly Holly melted into
his embrace before kissing the top of Helen's head. "Love
you both, even though you're a jerk. You too, Peanut. I'll
remember this when you're older."

A small chuckle escaped Ben before he pulled Holly in
tighter. He knew without a doubt he loved this woman
more than anything in the world. As he stood there with her
and Peanut in his arms, and knowing Jimmy and their fur
babies were playing somewhere in the house, life couldn't
get any better.

Ben sighed closing his eyes for a brief moment. When
he opened them, that's when he saw it. As he looked over
Holly's shoulder, he spotted the scorch marks on the wall,
causing a ridiculously wide smile to appear on his face.

The holidays were sure as hell gonna be fun this year.

"You know, Grace, I was thinking maybe for Christmas
dinner you could work your magic and make the other wall
match? It sure would be a show for everyone invited. I know
John's already placing bets on what you'll set on fire."

Holly jerked back cocking her brow at him. "What?"

When Ben jerked his head toward the burn marks, a
deep growl escaped Holly as she narrowed her eyes at him.

"You and John can kiss my ass." She plucked Helen from his arms and stormed out of the room leaving a laughing Ben behind.

Yep, the holidays were going to be a blast.

CHAPTER TWO

"Oh boy, who twisted your panties in a bunch?" Mildred asked, casually strolling into the library early Saturday afternoon.

Holly's face snapped up before glaring at the old woman in disbelief. *Why is she here? Isn't today her day off?* Holly's eyes went to the ceiling. *Can I not catch a break, Universe?*

"Whoo-wee must've been bad. Your eye's already twitching. Who was it? No, no, wait let me guess. This could be fun." The glee on Mildred's face made Holly want to throw something at her head.

Mildred plopped her hip onto the desk tapping her chin with her finger. "My first instinct is to go with Ben, but with man meat like he's got, you couldn't stay mad at him long enough to still be mad here. Besides if it was him, he'd probably pound your lady bits so hard you'd forget why you were mad in the first place." Mildred winked as she pulled out the pad of paper she kept with her.

"Really?" Holly's brows arched at the old coot.

"Shh, I'm thinking. Now, I don't believe it'd be Jimmy.

That boy is sweeter than apple pie. Then there's my little munchkin of course, but what could she do to make you look like that?" Mildred waved her finger up and down at Holly's scrunched face. "Nothing. That little girl is only an angel." Mildred scribbled on her paper. "That leaves Waffles, Ripley, Twitch, and your dad. You know what, I'm going with Waffles. He probably stole a pair of your ripped panties that Ben so devilishly tore from your body the night before. I bet Waffles, the sly dog that he is, dropped them in the middle of the living room and everyone saw them. So now you're embarrassed." Mildred looked at her watch. "Hot damn, I'm good. I got to the bottom of this in less than five minutes. I should get an award."

Holly stared at her in awe. "Where do you come up with this stuff?"

"Don't be jealous I'm a mastermind. When the detective Mildred hat goes on nothing can stump me."

"Well, you're gonna need to go back to the true-crime section and read up, 'cause you're wrong." Holly crossed her arms over her chest as she sat back in her seat. "For your information, it was all of them."

Mildred's eyes shot open as her hand went over her chest. "No! Say it ain't so? Even my little munchkin?"

"Yes. Even your little munchkin." Holly rolled her eyes.

Mildred sat on the desk for a few moments as she thought it over before shaking her head. "Nope. My detective skills are telling me there is only one answer here."

Holly cocked her brow. Whatever the old woman had come up with would probably annoy her but she couldn't stop her next words as the sarcasm poured out of her, "Oh yeah, please enlighten me."

"Yep," Mildred popped the 'p'. "My conclusion is... it was your fault."

"How is it *my* fault? And why is everyone picking on me today?" A pout emerged on Holly's face as her brows pulled together. *Stupid family. Stupid Mildred. Stupid Waffles.*

"You're an easy target. What do you expect? Now, tell me what'd ya do that had even my little munchkin after you."

Holly's expression pinched together. "I don't know what the big deal is. I was just trying to do something nice for my family... That's it. It's not like I was going to burn down the house or anything. I was just gonna make some waffles for everyone. Is that a crime?"

Mildred snapped back in terror. "You were gonna cook?!"

"I *am* allowed to cook. I'm a grown-ass adult after all."

"No, you're not!"

"Am too. I'm married and have two kids. I *am* an adult." *Take that!*

"Sure, whatever, you're an adult, that's questionable but you are *not* allowed to cook." Mildred shuddered in horror as a new wave of disgust washed across her face. "I don't know why you'd even try to...Wait a second, now I get it." Mildred slapped her knee. "You wanted to see that hunky fireman again. *Now,* I understand it. He's the one that's come out to your house a couple of times when you cooked. Remember the chicken tenders? Whoo-wee, he sure is a fine piece of meat. I knew you wouldn't be stupid enough to actually cook." Mildred wiped her brow.

A deep growl came from Holly's throat as Mildred patted herself on the back. "I swear to God, Mildred, I will murder you."

"I don't blame you at all. That man sure is hot stuff. No wonder why he became a fireman." Mildred fanned herself.

"His cat is also one of my husband's patients, so can you stop? This has nothing to do with the fire department. Plus, that *hunky* firefighter told us the next time he needed to respond to the house he was taking our stove with him. So, no. And while we're at it, can you stop bringing that back up? Every time Hank or his wife brings Dog into the clinic, they *remind* me not to turn on the stove."

"That's right, you told me he's the one with the giant cat named Dog."

"Yes, that's the one. I really need to remember you never forget anything I tell you." Holly shook her head.

"He is pretty fine. Remember when I caught him and his wife in the back of the library?" Mildred got a faraway look in her eyes. "You know what, I think I should call the fire station and tell them Holly Richman's trying to cook her lunch in the break room. You and I both know he'll be the first one here."

As Mildred reached for the phone Holly snatched it from her. "You better not! I swear to all things I will murder you and no one will ever find your body."

"Oh, yeah, yeah, let's go with that one. That way Officer Jones can come by instead. He is f-i-n-e. I'm only seeing this as a win-win for me."

Holly threw her hands in the air. Today was not her day. "Why are you here anyway? It's a Saturday. You're normally off."

"My knitting club is getting together in a few hours and I needed some good material."

"So, you came here 'cause you knew I was working?"

"Duh, who else do I get the best stories from? My gal-pals live for your antics. You're their highlight of the week."

"Great, not only does my own family troll me, so does you and your stupid knitting club." Holly went back to searching the internet trying her best to ignore the crazed woman sitting on top of the desk.

"Let me get this straight, your family was making fun of you for cooking, and now you're here at work annoyed at them?"

Holly rolled her eyes. "A little. I'm not really annoyed, but I'm going to get them back for it. Especially, Ben."

"Really, how so?"

Holly turned the computer around to face Mildred. On the screen was a horde of holiday elf costumes. They were in all different sizes, colors, and shapes. They had every-thing from pointy ears all the way down to green pointy toe shoes with bells on them. Holly's smile widened as she thought of everyone dressed up. They'd probably grumble about it, but dang they would be adorable!

"I don't get it."

"Ugh." Holly's eyes flicked upwards. "Of course, you don't. I'm gonna make everyone dress the same for our holiday Christmas card."

"And that's a punishment?" Mildred cocked her brow.

"It will be when they realize they have to wear the pointy shoes and ears! That's what they get for making fun of me. Oh, and check this out..." Holly clicked through the site with the mouse. "They have the same costume for pets. I can get one for each of the dogs *and* Twitch. We're all gonna be Santa's little helpers' whether they like it or not." *And, I'll be damned if Waffles tries to fight me for putting clothes on him again.*

"And what did Ben have to say about it?"

"He doesn't know yet. And he isn't gonna say anything. This *is* happening. It's our first Christmas together as a whole family and this is what we're doing. And, so help me if any one of them tries to argue, I will bake them cookies and force them to eat 'em."

"You wouldn't?" Mildred's face held a repulsion Holly hadn't seen in a while.

"Try me."

Mildred held up her hands in surrender. "You sure are snarky. Christmas is only a few weeks away. Aren't you supposed to be all jolly and stuff? Did someone pee in your food this mornin'?" Mildred smirked. "Well, at least you didn't cook it."

Holly narrowed her eyes as her lips thinned. "I *am* jolly."

"If you call that jolly, then I'm Mother Teresa."

"*I am jolly*. Can't you see it on my face?" Holly pointed at herself. "See, ho, ho, ho, and all that shit."

"Sure, you're super jolly and festive right now. I see the holidays coming out of your ears." Mildred rolled her eyes.

"I am damn it. It's Jimmy's first Christmas with us and Helen is here now. I'm gonna make this the most perfect Christmas anyone has ever seen and I will kill anyone that ruins this for me. You hear me?"

"Hold your horses there, tiger."

"No. I need this to be good for everyone. Jimmy deserves the world and so does Helen. Poor Jimmy has been through enough and I never want him to feel the way he did ever again. Not to mention, this is Peanut's *first* Christmas. So, it *has* to be special for both of them. I won't accept anything else."

"It will be. Relax. You're stressing yourself out when really you need to be enjoying the season. Instead, you're here hate buying stupid elf costumes for some Christmas card you won't get out in time."

Holly's mouth dropped at Mildred's statement. "How could you?"

"You know I'm right, and good luck getting Henry in one of those things." She pointed at the screen.

"My dad will stuff his butt into a costume or he'll have to suffer my wrath."

"Okay there, killer. Got it. Just make sure I'm around or at least record it for me. I don't want to miss that." Mildred softened as she looked at Holly, sighing. "You're trying to make this Christmas the best holiday you can and you're putting too much pressure on yourself. You're gonna find out it's all too much and then you'll end up blowing up your kitchen...." Mildred nodded but then stopped. "Actually, that'll be good material. I'm here for it. Your meltdowns give me and my gal-pals endless entertainment. Carry on."

"You know what, you're no longer invited to Christmas Dinner."

Holly: one.

Mildred: zero.

"I'm still gonna show up."

She would too. "I'll have Waffles guard the door, so you can't come in."

"Like he's gonna leave the kitchen?" Mildred burst out into a deep laugh. "Man, you crack me up. My knitting club is going to eat this up tonight."

"You're knitting group can kiss my ass. This will be perfect and I will murder all of you to get it that way. Don't make me tell you again."

"So much violence. I think I'm gonna have to call Benny boy and tell him you need a good workout to deal with your aggression." She winked. "I'm sure he can *pound* some sense into you."

"Stop talking about my husband pounding me."

"Hey, it's not my fault you need to get laid."

"For your information, I got laid last night!"

Mildred quickly grabbed her pen and paper and eyed Holly. "Oh, really, tell me all about it."

"You're disgusting."

"No, I'm amazing and you're jealous."

"Why yes, of course, that's the answer. I'm jealous of a horny, million-year-old lady who talks too much."

"So, you admit you're jealous of me then? It's about time really. Now, we can move on from this and get to the good stuff. Like what happened last night."

"Mildred!" Holly threw a pencil at her head, but the crazy old bat caught it with ease.

"Thanks, my pen was running out of ink. I don't know what I'm gonna do with you, missy." Mildred shook her head as she shoved her pad back into her pocket.

"Put me out of my misery."

"Nah, then my knitting club would be boring." Mildred popped herself off the desk before turning back to Holly. "I'm glad we had this little chat. You've given me tons of stuff. Not to mention, you helped me hone one of my skills. I *knew* it was your fault. Told you I was a detective." Mildred sent her a smug look before she sashayed herself through the library headed toward the true-crime section.

"That's it, I'm getting you and your husband elf costumes too, and I'm gonna make you wear them!"

Mildred looked over her shoulder at Holly. "Oooh, sounds like fun. Maybe you should order me two pairs. I bet a little role play will be in order and I have no idea the state the first one will end up in once hubby gets his hands on me."

Holly physically gagged as she shuddered in disgust. "Mildred! There are people in here."

The old woman scanned the room and shrugged. "Maybe it'll give them some inspiration? The holidays are coming up, you know. Everyone can use a little spice in their life. Maybe that could be their gift to each other." Mildred glanced to the right where the true-crime section was and then to her left where the romance books were. "On second thought, I think I'm going to get some inspiration myself." With that, Mildred beelined it straight toward the romance section with an extra pep in her step.

Holly slammed her head on the desk. "Kill me now."

CHAPTER THREE

"WHY AM *I* BEING PUNISHED?" John grumbled as he kicked a plastic Christmas ornament across the floor. "I didn't piss off your wife. *You* did."

Ben rolled his eyes at his best friend as he tossed John a box of holiday decorations. "You piss her off all the time. Consider these brownie points in advance."

"True, but I still don't understand why *I* need to help you get decorations up. This isn't my house."

"You're coming for Christmas dinner, aren't you?"

"Depends who's cooking." John narrowed his eyes on Ben.

John was going to give Ben a migraine and he'd only been there an hour. "Me. Emma's bringing a few sides, and Mildred dessert."

At the mention of Emma's name, John's whole face lit. "Yeah, I'll be here."

Ben threw him another box that was marked *living room decorations*. "You talk too much and besides, didn't I promise you food?"

"The word food is what got me over here." John caught

the box.

"I know."

"Speaking of which, where the hell is my food?" John tapped his stomach after putting the box at his feet. "I'm hungry."

"You're always hungry." Ben opened a box taking out two decorative snowmen Holly liked placed at their front door. "I need your help to get everything done by the time Holly gets back from the library."

"Again, just cause you're in the dog house doesn't mean I need to be."

"Shut up and start unpacking that box."

John muttered something under his breath as he did what he was told. "I don't know why I put up with you. And where the hell is my food?"

"Here you go, Uncle John," Jimmy announced, walking out of the kitchen with a bag of potato chips in his hand.

Promptly, John snatched them from the boy. "At least someone loves me." With that, John opened the bag and put the corner to his lips as he dumped the contents into his mouth. When he finished he looked back at Jimmy. "Thanks, kid." John glanced at Ben with a smug expression on his face. "I'm his favorite."

Instantly, Jimmy grabbed the empty bag from John as he narrowed his eyes. "Maybe now you'll stop talking. My sister is taking a nap."

John's hand shot to his chest. "Right through the heart, kid. I'm supposed to be your favorite."

Jimmy shrugged as a goofy smile emerged on his face. "I brought you food, didn't I?"

John snapped his attention to Ben with his brow cocked. "You sure he didn't come from you? 'Cause he acts exactly like you."

Ben laughed as Jimmy winked at him. He wondered that same question at times.

"That's 'cause I want to be just like my dad when I grow up."

Ben's heart stopped. He'd never get tired of hearing that. Since the moment they met at the dog park, Jimmy had always said the same thing. Ben's face softened as he watched his son. "I'll teach you everything you'll ever need to know."

"You sure about that?" John waved his hand up and down pointing at himself. "Why not be a dentist like your favorite uncle?"

"Eww. I don't want to be a dentist."

At the horror on Jimmy's face, John jumped back as his hand went to his chest like he'd been shot again. "Eww. Really, kid? Are you really gonna say eww? If it wasn't for my expertise your mother would have half of her tooth gone. I'm a hero." John puffed out his chest.

"Mom would've looked pretty even with a chipped tooth."

Ben's eyes sparkled as the two bickered. "She did look adorable with it."

"Whatever. I'm a hero." John tossed a Santa hat at Ben's head.

"You touch people's mouths all the time. That's kinda gross." Jimmy shuddered.

"Yeah, and your Dad has to examine animal poop. Whose job's grosser now?" John straightened his shoulders clearly happy he thought he'd won.

However, both Ben and Jimmy eyed each other before shifting back at John. "You," they replied at the same time.

"I get zero respect here," John scoffed before turning

back to the box of decorations. "Being a dentist isn't gross. The mouth fascinates me."

"Why?" Jimmy asked, cocking his head to the side as he pondered it. "Why would the mouth fascinate you?"

A huge smile spread across John's face. "I'll tell you when you're older."

Ben laughed before grabbing a piece of garland from one of the boxes. He knew exactly what was coming next.

Jimmy only waited about five more seconds. "I'm older now, can you tell me?"

John shot his eyes to Ben before looking back at Jimmy at a loss for what to say.

"I'm even older now. Every second that goes by I'm older. So, which older is it? Right now older or in a minute older? I'm wasting away here as I keep getting older."

"Ben, a little help here?"

"He's right you know. My boy's a smart one."

"He didn't get that from you." John narrowed his eyes before turning back to Jimmy. "Once you're *way* older you'll realize just how fun mouths can be."

"And that's enough of that!" Ben jumped to his feet. "Jimmy, will you help me put the garland on the mantel? Mom will be super happy to see it all done when she gets home."

"Sure!" Jimmy shouted forgetting about their conversation as he ran to the garland. As Ben caught John's eye, he sent him a death glare.

"What? I was talking about kissing."

"Sure, you were." Ben tossed him back the Santa hat. "Put this on so you can look the part."

"You sure are demanding." John flung the hat down the hall. "I have no idea why Holly puts up with you."

The corner of Ben's lips quirked up. "She likes my

mouth."

John gagged. "And you say *I'm* bad."

"You *are* bad." As Ben held up the right side of the garland to the mantle, Waffles waddled into the living room with the discarded Santa hat in his mouth. "That's the spirit, Waffles. Show Uncle John how much of a humbug he is."

The Corgi plopped onto his belly as he nibbled on his newfound treasure, causing John to raise his brow at the dog. "How is that the spirit? He's chewing on it."

Jimmy ran to the box in the corner labeled *Holiday Dog Clothes*. "No, he's not. He's asking for someone to put it on him." Jimmy rifled through the box until he found the dog Santa hat with the holes for ears and strap to go under his chin.

Once Jimmy grabbed the hat he ran back to Waffles. Before anything could happen, Ben tried to stop him. "I don't think that's a good idea, Kiddo. Last year when your mom tried to put that hat on him, he almost killed her. He's feisty when it comes to clothes now."

"I know what Waffles wants, Dad." Jimmy carefully took the hat and placed it on the dog's head before securing the elastic under his chin. "There, see? Look how cute he is! Mom's gonna love it."

Ben stood there in awe as Waffles let Jimmy maneuver his ears so they would fit perfectly in the holes. However, the moment Waffles' eyes caught Ben's, he saw the annoyance. "Don't look at me that way. I told him you don't like to be dressed up anymore."

Waffles sent Ben a glare before he barked. Then to prove Ben wrong he turned back to Jimmy jumping into his lap to lick his face. "Seems like he likes it just fine to me, Dad."

That bastard. Ben stared at the betraying dog. *Wait until Holly hears about this. Actually, never mind. I'll never hear the end of it. This will have to be our little secret.*

A deep laugh came from John as he watched the two playing on the floor. "Seems like Waffles only listens to one person in this house."

Waffles looked at John huffing before going back to Jimmy.

"And it sure as hell ain't you." Ben shook his head with a chuckle.

"Whatever."

Ben decided to ignore John as his eyes scanned around the room at all the decorations scattered everywhere. It was like the North Pole had thrown up. He quickly glanced down at his watch. They still had a lot more to do before Holly got home. He thought back, he couldn't remember if today was a half-day for her or a whole day. He really needed to get a move on if he planned on having everything done in time. "You two start putting up the tree. I'm gonna grab the last few boxes from the attic."

"Okay!" Jimmy sprinted to the box with the tree in it, dropping his end of the garland on the floor. "Come on, Uncle John. Let's put up the tree!" The excitement from Jimmy was almost more than Ben could take. "This is going to be the best Christmas ever. I can already feel it."

Ben's heart flipped. *I'll do everything I can to make sure of that, kiddo.*

"Yeah, yeah." John dropped a stuffed Santa on the floor which Waffles gladly ran over to and started chewing on. "The sooner we get this done. The sooner we get to eat."

"You just ate a whole bag of chips."

"And you think that's gonna last me?"

Jimmy studied him for a moment, as he cocked his head

to the side. "No."

"Exactly."

Ben chuckled as he watched the two of them. At least it was entertaining. As Ben looked around the room again, he saw just how much they still needed to do.

He knew Holly really wanted to make this Christmas special for everyone, he got it. He wanted to as well. This was their first Christmas as a family, and he wanted it to be perfect for all of them just as much as she did.

He wanted these memories to last a lifetime.

A ridiculously wide smile spread across Ben's face. Although, Thanksgiving was a memory they'd never forget. From where Ben stood, he could see the tail end of the scorch marks on the wall. "You two get the tree started. I'll be right back with the rest of the stuff."

"Sure thing, boss." John patted his stomach. "But first, it's time for a snack. Come on, Jimmy, if we've gotta keep working we need food."

"You just ate." Jimmy ignored him as he fussed with the box that had the tree in it.

"Not enough."

Ben rolled his eyes as he made his way down the hall. Leave it to John to always make things difficult.

As Ben walked past the last door, he did a quick peek into the nursery to see Peanut still fast asleep in her crib with Ripley and Twitch curled up on the floor next to it.

That kid can sleep through anything, he chuckled to himself. He didn't know where she got it from, but he was thankful for it. Especially, when John was in the house.

As quietly as he could, Ben shut the door so that it was only a quarter of the way open. He then headed to the hatch for the attic a little farther down the hall.

The moment he got the ladder down, though, he saw

Twitch had migrated out of the nursery to see what he was up to. As his little head twitched the cat looked around before his eyes went back to Ben.

"Your guess is as good as mine."

Twitch's attention darted toward the kitchen as the distinct sound of a bag opening rang through the hall.

"You're Uncle John's here." Ben chuckled. "If you hurry you might get a scrap of food before he eats it all. Waffles is already in there."

Twitch looked at him for one more second before he took off running toward the kitchen causing Ben to let out a laugh.

Never a dull moment.

Once Ben got into the attic, he crawled over to the last two boxes of decorations. As he walked carefully across the beams, he made a mental note to eventually put in a floor up there, so he wouldn't have to worry about stepping on the wrong part.

Lord knows the disaster that would happen if Holly ever got a wild hair across her ass and decided to go into the attic.

There would be no question about it.

That *would* be a disaster.

As Ben grabbed the two boxes, stacking one on top of the other he took a step back toward the hatch only for his heart to stop.

At that exact moment, he heard the distinct sound of their front door slamming open, and one angry Holly yelling, *"What the hell is going on here?"* echo through the house.

Unfortunately for Ben, the jolt somehow made him lose his footing as he slipped.

Before he knew it, Ben was falling through the ceiling.

CHAPTER FOUR

HOLLY THANKED the Universe today was only a half-day at the library. Especially after Mildred showed up. She wanted nothing more than to go home and relax. Holly wasn't really angry anymore; she was just stressed.

She really did want everything to be perfect. She knew she needed to take a step back and breathe. But it was hard.

A mischievous smile spread across her face as she walked up the steps of her home. She'd be lying if she said she wasn't excited to show all the traitors what outfit they'd be wearing for their Christmas card.

Her smile grew wider as she thought about it.

Holly even paid for expedited shipping so everything would arrive on Monday.

And no one was gonna argue with her about it. Everyone was going to dress up and be happy or they'd have her to deal with.

Her eyes narrowed.

That went for Waffles too. Ripley didn't mind wearing clothes but every time Holly tried to dress Waffles, he'd lose his mind.

Clearly, the jerk now thought clothes were beneath him.

Not this year, though.

That asshole was gonna wear his elf costume whether he liked it or not!

As Holly opened the door her eyes nearly popped out of her skull as the wind was almost knocked out of her. It was like a bomb had gone off in her living room.

A Christmas bomb. One that left nothing but destruction and sparkles in its wake.

There were ornaments all over the floor. One of which was being batted around by Twitch. Waffles was chewing on the Santa plush doll Holly had bought for Ben last year. There were boxes knocked on their sides with lights, garland, and decorations spilling out. You name it, it was happening.

Then to top it off, their Christmas tree was in pieces scattered all over the room. "What the hell is going on in here?"

Before Holly could take another step into the living room though, a loud crash rang throughout the room.

Then there was Ben.

Holy crap on a freaking cracker!

Her husband was now in their living room surrounded by pieces of their ceiling and insulation. Thank all the things he miraculously ended up somehow on their couch.

As Holly raced over to her husband to make sure he was okay, John stormed out of the kitchen a sandwich in his hand. "Holy shit."

Holly ignored John as she skidded to her knees next to Ben. "Are you okay? Please tell me you're okay?"

"I'm fine," he answered, dazed as he blinked a few times.

"Are you sure?" Holly's heart raced as she checked all

around and other than the colossal mess that was now everywhere, Ben seemed to be okay. He was extremely lucky he ended up where he did. Oh my God, she was going to have a heart attack. This was it.

This was her moment.

Might as well say goodbye now.

"Dude, you fell through your ceiling." John took another bite of his food as he laughed.

"Did I?" Holly watched as Ben's eyes scanned around the room before glancing up to the giant hole that now resided in their living room.

"Yes, you did!" Holly's heart officially stopped. "What the hell, Ben?"

"Everything is fine." He sat up slowly brushing off the insulation from his body.

"Everything is fine?" Holly's eyes widened at his nonchalant attitude. "*Everything is fine?*"

"Yeah," he replied, his eyes squinting at their ceiling.

Something inside of Holly snapped. "Everything is *not* fine! Ben, you just fell through the ceiling."

Ben did a once-over of his body again. "I really am okay. I'm not hurt at all and I didn't break anything." He patted his ribs to double-check. "Whoa."

"You're lucky 'cause you're about too." Holly punched him in the arm. "Don't ever scare me like that again!"

"Scare you?" He cocked his brow. "I'm the one that fell, not you."

Holly ignored him as she continued, "And you you wanted to wrap *me* in bubble wrap! I should wrap *you* in bubble wrap! I've never fallen through a ceiling before. Who needs to be accident proofed now?" Holly looked up once again. "Holy crap, look at that hole!"

Ben groaned as he rolled his eyes. "You've never fallen through the ceiling 'cause I don't allow you up there."

John burst out laughing in that can't control it double over in pain kind of laugh. "Holy shit, dude, you fell through the ceiling. This is the best day of my life. I take it back. I don't know why I was complaining about being here. I would've missed this if I wasn't." John laughed harder gasping for air.

As John continued his roaring, Jimmy slowly walked over to the couch his eyes wide as tears threatened to fall from them. "Dad, are you okay?"

Still a little shaken, Ben reached for their son. "Yeah, I'm okay, Jimmy. Thankfully, I landed on the couch."

Jimmy looked him over before letting out a small breath. "Do we need to take you to the hospital, like we have to take Mom sometimes?"

Holly gasped as she frowned at the little jerk who was sporting a shit-eating grin on his face. "It's been months since I've been to the ER."

Jimmy shifted toward Holly. "That's 'cause Dad can patch you up at the clinic."

Holly's mouth fell open. *Oh my God, how did this get turned back onto me again? I didn't just fall through the freaking ceiling!*

"This is priceless." John laughed harder. "Only thing that'd make it better, is if I had popcorn."

Holly snapped her attention to John. "Shut your pie hole or I'll shut it for you." Might as well call Officer Jones 'cause Holly was going to lose it.

A goofy smile appeared on John's face as his brows shot up. "With pie?"

Holly growled deep in her throat. "If by pie, you mean my fist, then yes."

Just as Holly was about to lose it, Ben took her in his arms. "He's not worth it."

"Am too," John announced.

They both ignored him as Ben continued to hold Holly in his arms. The fact he was okay made her relax but at the same time she wanted to scream.

Holy shit!

Her adrenaline hadn't been this high since Jimmy disappeared at the hospital while she was giving birth to Helen.

Holy fucking shit.

Who falls through the ceiling? That shit only happens in the movies... Then she thought about it. Actually, that *would* happen to them.

Holly took another deep breath as she pulled back from Ben's arms giving him another once-over. He really did look okay.

Thank the Universe.

Then Holly's eyes looked around the room again, mess wasn't even close to what it really was. Over in the corner, she saw Twitch climbing through one of the holiday boxes. She shifted back to Ben. "Why were you putting up the decorations? I thought we were going to do that tomorrow as a *family*."

Maybe it was the adrenaline of watching her husband fall through their ceiling, but somehow, a pang of hurt rang through her. Holly wanted to put up the decorations together. To make a memory that would last a lifetime. And to make sure it was perfect, of course.

"We were trying to surprise you, Mom."

"This sure is a surprise all right." Holly sighed, pulling Jimmy into her arms kissing him on the head. He might be a traitor but she loved him. Subconsciously, her eyes glanced at the hole again. *I can't believe this is happening.*

"Dad, why did ya have to fall through the ceiling?"

"It wasn't my plan."

Jimmy looked at the hole and then back to him. "That's a big hole."

"That's what she said." John burst into another round of hysterics as he laughed at his own joke.

"John!" Holly jerked her eyes to him.

"What?"

Holly shook her head before she turned back at her husband. "It's okay. No one is hurt." Out of nowhere, Holly couldn't help the smirk that appeared on her face as the thought jumped through her head. "Are you sure you're okay, *Grace?*"

"Oh, no you don't. The only Grace in this relationship is *you.*" Ben's brows shot up as he stared at her.

"And yet, I've never fallen through the ceiling."

"'Cause you're not allowed up there, I just told you that! Besides, I wasn't the one who tried to burn down the house this morning."

Holly's jaw dropped as her eyes narrowed on her husband. "I hope the size I ordered is too small."

Ben cocked his head to the side as he stared at her. "What?"

"Mom, Dad," John sarcastically remarked, interrupting them. "This is all fun and games, but is someone gonna feed us?" He pointed at Jimmy. "He's a growing boy and needs all the food he can get."

Jimmy darted his head to John. "You just ate."

"Okay, fine. *I'm* a growing boy." He patted his stomach again.

Holly threw her hands in the air as she jumped to her

feet. "You know what? Everything is fine. It's fine. It's all fine." Holly did her best to avoid the land mines on the floor as she walked to the nursery leaving the mess behind her. When she opened the door, she saw a still sleeping Helen in her crib with Ripley standing guard ready to do whatever she needed to in order to protect the baby.

Go figure. That kid would sleep through an earthquake.

"At least you aren't a pain in my ass." Gently Holly woke Peanut after grabbing the baby bag and made her way back into the living room.

Ben stood by the fireplace still brushing the insulation off himself as John continued to laugh his ass off. How in the hell had her day ended up here? She would have looked to the ceiling to curse the Universe but then that would involve her seeing the hole again.

Instead, Holly scanned the room and as she did, she once again saw Waffles chewing on the plush Santa doll.

Wait a second... This time she got a better look at her dog.

Holy shit, Waffles had *the* Santa hat on! Holly's eyes widened. "Is he wearing the hat I got him? Who got him to agree to that?"

"I did," Jimmy answered with a toothy grin on his face. "He asked me to put it on him."

Holly's eyes narrowed at the dog. "He asked you?"

Then to no one's surprise, Waffles sent Holly the biggest side-eye that she'd ever seen.

"Yeah, he asked me to."

Holly's eyes narrowed further on her dog as she recalled the pain in the ass he was last year as she tried to put that same hat on him. "And he just *let* you do it? There were no arguments?"

"None. He wanted it. See, look how cute he is. I'm

gonna go through the box again and find Ripley's so they can match."

"You do that," she answered, not taking her eyes off of her betraying dog. "You are going on Santa's naughty list."

"No, you're not!" Jimmy hollered. "Don't listen to her, Waffles. You're on the good list."

A deep growl escaped Holly as her jerk of a dog turned his nose up at her.

That's it.

A person can only take so much in one day.

"You know what, I'm going to Emma's." Holly hiked the baby bag higher on her shoulder making sure to keep Helen securely in her arms. "And when I get back this better be fixed." She pointed at John. "You go get my dad so he can supervise."

"Me?" John cocked his brow at her. "What the hell? I didn't fall through the ceiling. Don't spit fire at me."

Holly gave him a look that dared him to cross her. "Do it."

John folded his arms over his chest. "Only if you tell Emma I said hi."

"I'll tell her you tried to kill my husband by pushing him through the ceiling."

"That works." John shrugged as he winked at her.

That only served to annoy Holly more. "Go get my dad and have all this cleaned up by the time I get home."

"What is it with all you Richman's being so demanding? I don't know why I stick around."

"You love us," Jimmy chimed in. "Stop complaining and let's go get Grandpa!"

As Holly took another calming breath, Ben walked over to her before kissing her on the head and then doing the same to Peanut. "As you wish."

"Don't you go throwing my favorite movie quotes at me." Holly's left eye twitched.

Ben smirked once more as he kissed the top of her head one more time. "Love you, Grace. Don't worry, we'll have this all cleaned up and back to normal in no time."

"Back to normal?" she scoffed. "There is no such thing as normal in this house."

Holly did another once-over of Ben who seemed completely fine. So fine in fact, that Jimmy, John, and Ben all sported the same stupid happy expression on their faces.

Oh God, she lived in a circus.

Even though her heart still raced at a dangerous level, somehow, Holly relaxed seeing Ben wasn't in immediate danger. Maybe it was because Helen was still fast asleep in her arms. Who knew?

There was only one thing Holly knew for certain. She was getting her ass out of there and by the time she got back, there should *not* be a hole in the ceiling.

How was this her life?

"I promise, you'll never know what happened." Ben winked.

Holly eyed him one more time before a smirk appeared on her face. "Make sure of it, *Grace.*" With that, she walked out of the front door.

CHAPTER FIVE

"SEE, GOOD AS NEW." Henry puffed his chest the best he could as he stared at the ceiling where the hole once was.

"You didn't do anything," John grumbled, frowning at Holly's dad like he had two heads.

"What do you mean I didn't do anything? I made sure you numb-nuts didn't screw it up," Henry squared off with John.

Ben rolled his eyes as he rubbed his side. It was pretty sore. After all he did fall through a ceiling *and* patched it back up.

"And we finished putting up all the decorations. Well, most of them," Jimmy announced with a smile. "Mom's gonna be so happy. She's been kinda cranky."

"That's my Pumpkin," Henry answered. "She goes a little overboard at times. Last week when you all came over, she was going ten million miles an hour. I still don't know how she ended up on her butt in the middle of the kitchen."

Ben and Jimmy both spoke at the same time, "She tripped."

"Figured as much." Henry laughed as he sent them his lopsided grin. "Like I said, she's a little crazy at times."

Ben smiled at his father-in-law, a man he now considered like his own father. "At times? How about all the time. And right now, even though she's got a screw loose. We still love her."

"True."

Henry cautiously sat on the couch as Waffles took a running leap to sit with him. Poor guy didn't make it, though. Instead, he hit his chest and fell back onto the floor. Just as Waffles was about to sulk away, Jimmy ran over to him.

"Here ya go." Jimmy picked Waffles up putting him on the couch. Instantly, Waffles eagerly cuddled up to Henry asking for belly rubs, plopping onto his back with his tongue hanging out of the left side of his mouth.

Figures.

"I ain't got any food, Waffles. You're barking up the wrong tree."

At that, Waffles huffed before he jumped off the couch giving Henry an evil glare as he trudged away toward the kitchen. "That dog's a piece of work."

"That's the nicest he's been all day." Ben laughed at the side-eye Waffles was now giving Henry. "Thanks for helping, Dad."

"Anytime, son. It was good to get out of the house. It's lonely there sometimes." Henry shuffled in his seat as a puppy dog expression appeared on his face before looking at Jimmy. "All by my lonesome."

Ben knew what was coming next. He'd been around his father-in-law enough times to know exactly what he was hinting at.

"Lonely? You shouldn't be lonely, Grandpa. Maybe I

can have a sleepover? We haven't had one of those in a really long time. It could be so much fun and then you wouldn't be so lonely." Jimmy looked at Ben. "Can I, Dad?"

"You come over here all the time, Henry. Not to mention, you talk to Holly or me every day." Ben sent Henry a look, which Henry promptly ignored. Henry then clapped his hands together in excitement eyeing Jimmy. "Why who would've thought of such a wonderful idea?"

"Me!" Jimmy jumped up and down.

"You are so smart. I think you take after me."

"Kid, you just got played," John remarked, rolling his eyes at Jimmy. "I thought I taught you better than that?"

Henry stared John down. "Not as played as you'll be when you find out you have to stop and buy us pizza on the way home."

John's face brightened at the words. "Joke's on you. I was planning on getting second dinner tonight when I dropped you off anyway."

"Yay, second dinner!" Jimmy bounced on his toes in excitement.

Oh God, Holly was going to kill him. "Just don't tell your mother."

"Speaking of Pumpkin. When is she coming home? I wanna see my little Peanut." Henry glanced at his watch. "It's not right for a grandpa to come all the way over here not to see his little grandbaby." Henry narrowed his eyes on Ben. "Took you long enough to give me both of them."

Ben didn't know whether the pain in his neck was from the fall or having to deal with John and Henry all day. "You got your grandbabies, didn't you?" Ben pulled out his phone. "Her text said any minute now. She left Emma's a little while ago."

"That Emma is a good one." A lopsided grin appeared on Henry's face.

"That she is," John mumbled.

As if on cue, the front door opened to reveal Holly and a smiling Peanut happy to be in her mother's arms.

"There they are!" Henry's whole face lit up.

Ben watched Holly's eyes jump to the ceiling before she acknowledged her dad. "Oh, whoa! Look, Peanut, it's like it never happened. Well, other than the smell of fresh paint."

"Nothing did happen. I told you we'd take care of it," Ben joked, walking over to his wife and baby. He quickly gave her a kiss on the lips before kissing their baby on the head.

"Only 'cause I was here to supervise. That idiot almost made another hole."

John snapped his eyes to Henry. "I thought we agreed not to talk about that."

"I didn't agree to shit."

Ben ignored the two children as he grabbed Holly's attention. "How was your day, Sweetheart?"

"It was good. I no longer want to strangle anyone if that's what you're asking. How are you feeling?" She studied his body up and down. "Are you hurting?"

Ben's eyes darkened. "If I say yes, will you kiss the spots I point to?"

"Told ya the mouth was awesome," John chimed in, turning to face Jimmy.

"What?"

"Nothing," John answered Holly before turning back to Jimmy with a wink.

Clearly deciding it was best to leave it alone for now, Ben watched as Holly focused wholeheartedly on her father. "Hey, Dad."

As Henry tried to get up, Holly stopped him. "No, it's okay I'll bring her to you." Holly moved over to her father before carefully placing Helen in his arms.

Henry ecstatic he held his grandchild in his lap, cooed at her. "There's my girl. I missed you today." Peanut's face brightened as she listened to her Grandpa speak.

Before anyone else could say anything, John spoke. "Yeah, yeah, hi Holly, how ya doing? Great. Glad you had fun and don't want to kill anyone anymore. How's Emma? Did she say anything about me? Did you talk about me? Did I come up at all?"

John talked so fast Ben's head spun.

"You sure did." Instead of elaborating, Holly glanced around the room. "Wow, it looks really good in here."

"Thanks! We worked really hard. As Uncle John and Dad fixed the ceiling, Grandpa Henry and I decorated. We left the Christmas ornaments for us to do together, though. Dad said we needed to do that as a family or you'd make him sleep on the couch."

"Aww, that was sweet of him and also correct." Holly kissed the top of Jimmy's head. "Thank you."

"Excuse me!" John interrupted.

"What?"

"What did you and Emma say about me? You can't just leave it at that. I need to know."

Holly got this mischievous spark in her eyes. "Oh, nothing. Or at least nothing to worry your little head about."

John's brows shot up. "What's that supposed to mean?"

Holly's smile went from ear-to-ear. "Exactly what I said."

"Really, after all I did today, you're just gonna leave me hanging like that? I thought I was your favorite."

"Nope." Holly shook her head. "Definitely not my favorite."

"Boy, if I were you I'd quit while you're ahead." Henry bounced Helen on his good knee.

As John realized he was going to lose this battle, he grumbled as he kicked a dog toy on the ground. Holly's eyes followed the toy as it landed at Waffles' feet. Who was staring at everyone in the room like they were the enemy. "Who pissed him off?"

"That would be me," Henry answered with a lopsided grin on his face. "He thought I had food and I didn't."

"That would do it." Holly eyed her Corgi. "Didn't we go over this already? No more treats. You're on a diet."

At the word diet, Waffles fell onto his back in a dramatic show as he whined.

"Nope, not gonna happen." Holly stood her ground.

Waffles grudgingly got up and huffed as he made his way down the hall, but not before swinging his head back at Holly with daggers in his eyes.

"Glad I don't have to deal with that tonight." Jimmy watched as the annoyed Corgi grumbled as he walked away.

"What do you mean you don't have to deal with that?" Holly turned back to Jimmy cocking her head. "Are you kicking him out of your room tonight?"

Jimmy's whole face lit. "Nope! I'm havin' a sleepover with Grandpa tonight and we're gonna get second dinner!"

"I thought we agreed you wouldn't tell her?" Ben groaned as he rolled his eyes. "I don't even know why we bother. No one can ever keep their mouth shut around here."

"That so?" Holly gave Ben a cross look.

"Yep, Uncle John is gonna take us to get more food before he drops us off at Grandpa's."

"Hmm." Holly stared John up and down before turning her glare back on Ben.

"Yeah, the old man played the kid and pretended to play me, but joke's on him. I'm always hungry."

"We know," everyone in the room said at the exact same time.

"Speaking of which, as much as I'd love to kiss up on my baby some more, it's time for us to head home. We got a fun night planned with movies and snacks!" Henry kissed the top of Helen's happy face one more time.

"Did you say snacks?" John's eyes widened at the word. "You know what, my plans have just changed. Jimmy, how would you feel if you're favorite uncle crashed your sleepover?"

"You just want the food," Jimmy answered, giving John the once-over.

"Yeah." John shrugged not denying it. "But we also get to watch movies together. I'll even let you watch the ones your mom and dad won't let you see."

Jimmy's face lit with excitement as he turned to Henry. "I know he's a pain, but can he come too? Maybe we can stay up *all* night and watch movies and then John can make us waffles in the morning!"

Waffles barked from the hall.

"You can't have any, Lord Waffles. You have to stay here and protect Peanut," Jimmy shouted back which caused a cry and another huff to come from Waffles.

Henry glanced at John who had a puppy dog expression on his face. "You make good waffles?"

"I dabble."

"Fine," Henry muttered. "You're buying the snacks, though."

"That's good with me. I hope you're ready to have a whole concession stand at your house. Let's go."

"Make sure you get dad sugar-free candies," Holly remarked, staring down John.

"Sugar-free?" Henry scoffed. "I might be old, but I don't need sugar-free, young lady."

"Don't worry," John stated, beaming at Holly before winking at Henry. "I'll get the sugar-free candy." John pointed at his eye. "Did you see what I did there? The wink's 'cause I'm lying. We're getting the good stuff."

Holly cocked her head at John in awe. "I know you're smart. You have to be smart. You got through school and are a damn good dentist but man I wonder about you sometimes."

"You wonder about me?" John cocked his brow. "Your husband know about that?"

Holly gagged as John turned to Ben. "How are you okay with your wife fantasizing about me? I mean, I know I'm the better looking one out of the two of us, but I'm surprised." John spun back to Holly. "I have to let you down easy. My heart belongs to someone else." John had the gall to give Holly a sad expression.

"I think I'm gonna vomit."

John shook his head. "I know it's got to be hard to stomach me letting you down. It breaks my heart too. You do have an amazing as—"

"That's enough of that." Ben carefully grabbed his daughter from his father-in-law. "Go get your stuff together, Kiddo. John can bring you home tomorrow morning."

As Jimmy took off out of the room, Ben snapped at John. "You wanna go? You talk about my wife's ass one more time and you'll regret it. Don't forget I'm skilled with a scalpel."

John rolled his eyes. "Like you'd even get close to me."

"Boys, can you stop?" Holly pleaded. "I don't want another baby shower incident again."

John's eyes darkened as he glared at his best friend. "I had more clothespins than you and you know it. You stole that crown from me."

"I did no such thing. I won fair and square."

"You're a cheater!"

Before Ben could retaliate, Jimmy was back in the living room with his bag. "I was gone for two seconds."

John puffed out his chest. "You're lucky your kid came back. He just saved you from getting your ass beat."

"Pretty sure Dad can take you." Jimmy quickly kissed Helen on the cheek. "Be good, Peanut. I'll be back tomorrow and we can put ornaments on the tree together. Mom really wants to do that."

Helen babbled her answer before a tiny smile appeared on her face.

Instantly, Ben's annoyance with John melted away as he looked at his children. Okay, not all of his annoyance. The next time Ben got the opportunity he was going to trip John.

Jimmy placed another kiss on Peanut's head before running over to Holly giving her a hug. "Love you, Mom! Dad already said it was okay. We'll be back early tomorrow morning. I promise. Then we can do the tree."

"Love you too, baby." Holly hugged her son before kissing the top of his head.

Henry carefully got up from the couch before walking over to Holly. "Love you, Pumpkin. We'll be back tomorrow morning to help with the tree. Try not to let your husband fall through any more ceilings while we're gone."

"I can't make any promises."

"Time's a wastin," John shouted as he grabbed his stuff

before scratching Waffles on the head and then walking over to Ben giving Helen a quick kiss. "See ya tomorrow, little one. While I'm away, work on your mother for me, will ya? I need some details on Emma."

"Not gonna happen." Holly laughed.

As John ignored Holly, he darted his eyes to Ben. "You still owe me food."

"I bought you two meals today."

"And yet, I'm still hungry."

Ben rolled his eyes. Chaos, Ben lived in complete chaos one hundred percent of the time.

As Jimmy helped Henry out of the house John walked behind them pushing them along.

"Don't stay up too late!" Holly hollered after them.

"We won't!" John hollered back as he winked.

"We already know the wink means you're lying." Holly shook her head as her eyes flicked up.

John winked again.

"Oh, for Pete's sake." Holly walked out of the front door and onto the porch. "Be good all of you. And Jimmy you're in charge."

"Hey!" John and Henry shouted at the same time.

"What? He's the most responsible out of the three of you."

"My own daughter, how could you?"

"It was easy." Holly shrugged. "You tried to pull one over on me with the non-sugar free candy."

"Who cares who's in charge. Let's go, I'm wasting away to nothing." John jumped in the car.

With that, Jimmy helped Henry into the passenger seat before hopping into the back and before anyone knew it, John was peeling out of the driveway and was out of sight.

With a chuckle, Holly and Ben walked back into the house closing the door behind them.

Ben carefully watched as Holly surveyed the entire room. "You know what, I'm not really sure what happened here the last ten minutes but the ceiling looks good. You guys did a good job. Thank you."

Ben walked over to his wife, kissing her on the cheek. "You're welcome, babe. And guess what?"

Holly looked at Peanut as she answered. "What?"

"We finally have the house to ourselves." Holly gazed up at him as a wicked smile appeared on Ben's face.

"That we do."

"Let me go put Helen to bed and then we're gonna have a little chat." He gave her a knowing look making Holly's brow quirk up.

"Oh, yeah?"

"Yeah, after all, you left the house *twice* today angry. That's not gonna fly. You and I are gonna have ourselves a nice little chat, and then I'm going to throw you over the back of the couch and fuck your brains out." At Holly's shocked expression, he winked. "Thank God our Peanut sleeps through everything. I plan on using our night alone to my advantage."

With a pep in his step, Ben strolled down the hall with a happy Peanut in his arms, leaving Holly standing there with her mouth hanging open.

CHAPTER SIX

Holly was still in a complete daze from Ben's words, as she stood frozen in their kitchen while he put Helen to bed for the night.

However, as Holly's brain raced with the events of the day, along with what Ben had just said, something inside of her broke.

Yeah, so she'd left the house a few times angry.

That was okay.

It happens.

And well, in her defense, she did watch her husband fall through the ceiling. That would've been a lot on anyone.

Plus, they were putting the decorations up. That was something she was looking forward to doing as a family...

Okay, sure, maybe she'd been a bit of a jerk lately and got angry for really no reason at all. But well... Damn it. It was a lot of pressure to put on the perfect holiday celebration.

Was it so wrong for her to want everything to go off without a hitch? Was it so wrong for her to want to give

Jimmy a good memory? All she wanted to do was replace the horrible ones he'd been through.

Holly clamped her eyes closed as she fought off the tears. She couldn't stop the feeling that washed over her.

It was like everything was failing and all at once.

Why am I not the one putting Peanut to bed? Why am I standing here paralyzed when Ben swoops in to be the most perfect father again?

What is wrong with me?

She was failing as a mother.

Holly's chest tightened as the tears she tried to keep at bay finally fell.

Pull yourself together! Holly angrily pushed her tears away with the back of her hand. *This isn't helping the situation. And how are you going to pull off the perfect Christmas if you're over here having a pity party?*

Exactly, you aren't, so get it together.

"Sweetheart, no." Ben appeared out of nowhere cupping Holly's cheeks in the palms of his hands. "Don't cry, Grace."

At his words, she broke into uncontrollable sobs.

Instantly, Ben pulled her into his arms, holding her tight. "Shh, it's okay. It's okay."

"It's not!"

Ben drew back as he lovingly gazed at her. "It's always going to be okay. As long as we have each other we will get through anything."

More tears threatened to spill as she looked at Ben.

"Talk to me."

Holly shook her head.

"Holly, talk."

"It's stupid."

"If it's upsetting you, it's not stupid. What's going on?

50

Don't get me wrong, Grace, you're normally a little high-strung but not like this. Talk to me, baby. We promised each other we'd always talk through it." Ben leaned in kissing her on the lips before wiping away her tears with the pads of his thumbs.

"It's just..." Holly took a deep breath. "I feel like I'm failing again."

"Why?"

As Holly studied her husband's eyes, she saw the amount of love he held for her, ultimately making her feel even worse. "I have to make everything perfect."

"You are."

Holly shook her head. "I'm not. Every time I try to do something it ends up a mess. I freaking hate bought elf costumes. I almost burned our house down. Mildred told me I'm putting too much pressure on myself and the fact that she was right makes me really want to punch her."

Ben cocked his head to the side. "That's a lot to unpack. We'll get back to the hate costumes soon, but first, I can't believe I'm going to say this, but I agree with Mildred."

She gasped. "You can't. I'm your wife, you have to agree with me."

"And normally I do, but babe, you are putting too much pressure on yourself."

"I have to, Ben. This is Jimmy's first Christmas with us. Look at all he's dealt with in his life. I can't let this be a disappointment to him as well. I don't want to cause him any more pain than he has already been through."

"Holly..."

"And then it's Helen's first Christmas," she kept going. "I know she probably won't remember it but I have to try, okay? God forbid something happens to me like it did my mom and—"

"No," Ben interrupted her. "That's not gonna happen, Holly. Stop."

At his words, Holly burst into another round of tears.

"It's okay." He held her tighter as Holly let everything out. The stress she'd been feeling, the pain, the anger. All of it came out in the form of tears soaking through Ben's shirt.

And after what felt like an eternity, she finally managed a deep breath, before calming down.

"You feel better?" He kissed the top of her head.

Holly nodded as Ben wiped away the tears from her eyes. "That's good. Baby, you're just having a holiday breakdown. That's normal."

Holly stared at him, shocked.

"It is. It happens to most people. Especially people that try to control everything, and actually end up controlling nothing." He bopped her nose with his finger.

"Ben..."

"Hear me out. It's not about making everything perfect, Holly. It's about making memories. And we *are* making memories. Stressing yourself out as much as you are isn't going to work. You aren't enjoying the holiday season. Instead, you are two seconds from strangling everyone you come in contact with."

"Am not."

Ben cocked his brow at her.

"Okay, fine. Maybe a little," she huffed.

When Ben didn't say anything Holly's brows knitted together. "Whatever, mister, you just jumped to the top of the strangle list."

The corner of Ben's mouth quirked up as he winked at her. "That could be fun."

"Ben," she growled as a chuckle escaped her at his attempt to lighten the mood.

"See, laughing is better than anger."

Holly took another calming breath, knowing Ben was right. Plus, it felt good to finally get all of this off her chest. It'd weighed her down, which only ended up causing *more* stress on her. "I guess. It's just I really do want to make everything special."

"And you are. Holly, our kids love you." The palm of Ben's right hand rested on the small of her back pushing her closer to his body. "They are happy, healthy, and loved. You already make them feel special." Ben placed his other hand under her chin, making Holly look directly into his eyes. "You're an amazing mom, Holly Richman. I'm proud of you."

As she looked at him, she felt his words.

She knew he was right. Jimmy always told her how happy he was and that he loved her and Helen.

Well, Helen was the perfect little baby. Holly still couldn't believe how well-behaved and happy she was. Then there was Ben. The love of her life. Something inside of Holly relaxed as she watched him. Ben always made things better. She might be in the midst of losing her mind, but somehow, Ben always brought her back down to reality.

Plus, he really was right. It wasn't about making the holidays perfect. It was about making memories.

Memories were what we'd take with us as we grow older through the years, and trying to force everything to be a certain way is only a recipe for disaster. What kind of memories would those bring back years later?

An annoyed Holly and a miserable Christmas. *That's what.* She wanted to punch herself.

Holly shook her head as she really took a moment to let everything sink in. As long as they had each other and their family nothing else really mattered. Thankfully, she would always have her Adonis to remind her. A soft smile formed on her lips. "I love you, Ben."

"I love you, too, Holly." He kissed her on the lips before pulling back. "You good now?"

"I can't make any promises," she answered. "But I'll try my best."

"That's all anyone could ask for." As Holly relaxed in his arms, a cocky smirk appeared on his face. "Do you want to tell me about hate buying elf costumes now?"

"Ugh..." Holly pushed back before grabbing her phone out of her pocket. "Those stupid hate costumes cost me over three hundred dollars."

"Huh?" He cocked his brow.

Holly shoved her phone in his face. "When I was at work, I found these elf costumes that I bought for all of us. It's gonna be our Christmas card. I thought it would get you all back for making fun of me."

Ben looked at the photo as an ear-to-ear smile emerged on his face. "You're gonna look hot as fuck in that."

"What? No." Holly's eyes nearly popped out of her skull. "You're not supposed to say that, you're supposed to be annoyed and fight me on it."

Ben glanced at the costumes again as his eyes darkened, filling with heat. "Why would I be annoyed? Do you see how short and fluffy this skirt is? It's gonna take everything in me not to rip you out of it."

Holly took a step back, causing her lower back to hit the counter. "No. No. You are not gonna turn this around. These outfits were gonna be my ultimate revenge. You are *not* supposed to get turned on by them. Do you see this? You even have to wear the pointy ears and the shoes with the bells on them."

"Sounds like fun." He took another step closer to her, boxing Holly in.

"You aren't supposed to like *this*." Her eyes narrowed.

"Holly, everything that involves you, I like. Haven't you figured that out yet?" He leaned in, kissing the side of her neck.

Holly's breath hitched as Ben nipped the skin causing heat to pool low in her belly. "Yeah, well. Uhh."

"It'll be fun." Ben kissed the bottom of her jaw. "I can think of all the scenarios I can put you in. What if I'm the Head Elf and I caught you slacking on the job? What are you gonna do so I don't tell the big guy?"

Holly's heart raced. Wait a second, no, this wasn't how any of this was supposed to go. "Ben..."

"That's Head Elf to you." Ben reached her ear, sucking the lobe into his mouth.

"You're not getting it. This is gonna be our *Christmas card*."

"I get it just fine," he replied, moving back to her jaw. "We'll be the most perfect elf family Santa has ever seen."

No, no, no. My plan cannot backfire.

"I bought one for each of our pets too."

"Good. Now, we'll all match."

Ben peppered kisses along her jaw as Holly continued, "And Mildred and her husband..."

"Okay." Ben's hands migrated to her hips pushing her body closer to his, so she could feel his length.

"And John and Emma..."

"That's fine.

"And my dad."

"Sounds good to me."

"Ben..."

"You're talking too much." With his words Ben effortlessly picked her up and placed her on the counter. "I'm picturing you in that costume and exactly what you're gonna have to do to prove you're serious about working at the North Pole." Ben's hands found the hem of Holly's shirt before escaping under it. As his fingers grazed her skin, her whole body trembled. His hands soon found their target as he cupped her chest. "I love these babies."

"You always say that."

"And I mean it." In a swift move, he pulled her top over her head before tossing it behind him. "I could get lost in these." He kissed the swell of her breasts causing a moan to escape from Holly's lips.

"Shh, little elf, you don't want the others to hear, do you? We have to keep things professional here in Santa's workshop." Ben's hands found the clasp of her bra, quickly releasing it.

And as Holly's chest bounced free, she smiled, cocking her head to the side. "And getting me topless is professional?"

"Extremely," he answered, moving in to kiss her right nipple, before bringing it into his mouth. As he worked her, his hands went to the waistband of her leggings. "Up."

"Up where?" She threw her head back as he tugged at her pants.

"Push your ass up. These are coming off." Without her even thinking about it, Ben had perfectly maneuvered her leggings so they slid down her legs, along with her panties.

Ben then instantly dropped to his knees once they were gone, tossing her right leg over his shoulder.

"Ben," she moaned. When she looked down, she saw Ben's lust-filled eyes staring back at her. "It's time for me to have my own Thanksgiving feast."

He took one long lick from bottom to top of her core,

making sure to keep his eyes on her as he did it. Holly's heart raced as her whole body heated at the sensation. "Not that I'm complaining, but how is this me proving I need to keep my job at the workshop?"

Just as Ben was about to suck her clit into his mouth he stopped, cocking his brow at her.

"Wait no, keep going." *Why did I have to say anything? Good going, dumb-dumb.*

"You're right." Ben stood, but not without taking another slow lick of her lower lips. "You're supposed to prove to *me* how bad you want to keep your job."

"Wait no, that's not—"

"Too late. You've already been extremely insubordinate, little elf. I'm gonna have to mark this down on your performance evaluation."

"My what? You have got to be kidding me."

"That's another mark." He playfully scolded her before leaning in to kiss her neck again.

"Ben..."

He pulled back cocking his brow at her. "That's Head Elf to you."

Holly rolled her eyes as she shook her head. "*Head Elf,* get back down there. You weren't done." She wiggled her hips trying to entice him.

Instead of falling for it though, Ben grabbed her hips dragging her off the counter. "Wrap your legs around me, you naughty little elf. It's time for your punishment."

"What the hell!" Holly did what he said or she would have ended up on her butt on the kitchen floor.

"And now you've said *hell*..." He shook his head. "You really are raking up the punishments. We do not curse here in Santa's workshop." Ben swatted her ass as he carried her through the house.

"Ben, I will—"

"Shh," he interrupted her as he bit down on her neck. "You don't want to wake anyone up. I heard Santa could be quite grumpy if he gets up too early. He needs to be rested for his big night."

"We are really doing this aren't we?"

Ben pulled back looking her in the face. "You sure don't know how to listen. You're just adding to the comment section in your evaluation, you know that right?"

Holly rolled her eyes again as Ben carried her down the hall toward their bedroom. "Are you gonna add in that you have me naked wrapped around you? Speaking of that, why am I the only one naked? This always happens. Why can't you be naked first?"

"You're prettier to look at than me."

"Says who?"

"Says me." Ben smacked her ass, before giving it a tight squeeze. "Now, stop talking or I'm adding that to the evaluation as well."

When Ben turned the corner into their room, he tossed Holly onto the bed before ripping his shirt off.

Damn, who knew role play could be this fun? Head Elf here I come.

"Ouch! What the crap?"

Instantly, Ben stopped from going to the belt buckle on his pants as he looked at Holly. "Why did you say ouch? I always toss you on the bed."

Holly ignored him as she jumped around on the bed before tossing their sheets back. When she held up one of their Christmas tree ornaments in her hand, he cocked his head to the side.

"What the hell is this?" She pulled out two more from under the pillow.

Ben continued to watch as Holly threw their sheets onto the floor at a loss for words. That's when he saw a whole stash of Christmas ornaments in all shapes and sizes on their bed.

"What the heck is going on here?" Holly picked up another one before looking at Ben.

"I don't know. I didn't put—"

"It was you!" Holly snapped her attention to the door.

As Ben turned his head, he saw none other than their special needs cat twitching his head from side-to-side as he held another ornament in his mouth.

Ben couldn't help but laugh as one of the cat's twitches was too strong, causing the ornament to fly through the air, landing on the floor in the middle of the room. Of course, the little guy then playfully ran after it, batting it around playing with his treasure.

"Are you bringing these up here?" Holly asked, holding up the ornament for Twitch to see.

As if to make matters worse, Waffles appeared from around the corner with his own ornament in his mouth. "You have got to be kidding me. What are you guys doing? Our bed is not your personal playground and these are not your toys!"

Waffles took the ornament in his mouth and tossed it at Holly before crouching down, playfully barking. "Oh, no, mister. We are *not* playing fetch."

At the word fetch, Ripley came running with another ornament in her mouth.

Ben burst out laughing, as his hand went to his stomach. *Holy shit, this is perfect.*

"Where in the heck are you guys getting these?"

Twitch batted the round ornament on the floor hitting Ben's foot. Ben watched the chaos around him as he kicked

59

the ball out of the door as a happy Twitch ran after it. "My guess is the box next to the tree."

Ben turned his attention back to Holly. The same Holly who was sending death glares to their pets as she held up a green and red sparkly tree ornament in her hand. "We do not play with these. They have enough toys. *These are not toys.*"

As she growled, Ben let out another laugh.

And Holly thought this holiday was going to be a disaster. Nope. From where I'm standing this shit is priceless.

Ben plucked the ball from Holly's hand before tossing it out of the room which had Ripley and Waffles happily running after it.

"Ben!"

"Let them have their fun, Grace." His eyes heated as he scanned her naked body up and down. "That way we can have ours."

Holly's breath hitched, but only for a second before she narrowed her eyes at him crossing her arms over her chest.

"You can argue with them later, Holly." His dick was already threatening to explode. "Little elf, right now you need to prove you've got what it takes to keep your job in Santa's workshop. Are you a good elf or a bad elf?"

"A good elf wouldn't let some whack-a-doo dogs and cat eat the ornaments." Holly cocked her left brow at him.

Ben's entire face brightened as a smirk formed on his lips. "And that's why you're one of the best elves here. But before I can let the big guy know that, you've got to prove it to me first."

"Prove what?"

Ben quickly unbuckled his belt before removing his pants and boxers from his body in one fast swoop. He couldn't help the pride that flared in his chest as Holly's eyes darted directly to his dick. No matter how many times she'd seen it, she'd always look at him like it was her first time.

"Thought so." He chuckled as he crawled up the bed toward her.

"Stop using your body to distract me."

"Now, you know how it feels." Ben separated Holly's legs as he moved in between them. "When you sway those hips of yours, I lose my fucking mind. Every time you walk into the room, I have to stop myself from throwing you over the closest surface and fucking you."

"That's not very Head Elf of you."

Ben's body heated as the corner of Holly's mouth turned up as she played back with him.

"I think that's exactly what the Head Elf should do. You've been teasing me all season long, little elf."

"I did no such thing." Holly moved her hands giving Ben better access to her body.

"And yet, my dick says otherwise." Ben grabbed the base of his member, positioning it at Holly's core.

"Your dick should be on Santa's naughty list then, not me." Holly arched her back welcoming him.

As Ben pushed the tip into her core, Holly's eye's closed. "Are you the one that's gonna tell him that?"

Holly's eyes shot open before she twisted her hips causing him to move. "And you said I talked too much. Shut your face and fuck me."

"That's another naughty word," he tsked, as he slowly pushed into her center. "What am I gonna do with you?" Holly arched her back giving him exactly what he wanted.

He loved the feeling of Holly wrapped around him. As her walls gripped his dick, pulling him into her body deeper, Ben thrust his hips, nearly losing himself in her heat.

Fuck, she was perfect.

Ben's hand migrated to her nub before rubbing in tight circles causing Holly to pant as she rolled her hips. "That's it, little elf. Give it to me."

"Please, more," she begged, sending a new shockwave of desire through Ben.

"Anything for you." He gritted his teeth as he moved faster, feeling his body tighten as he went. Holly met him thrust for thrust as he pushed himself harder into her core. Fuck, it was too much to handle.

As he felt her walls tighten around his dick, Ben pinched her clit. Instantly, Holly exploded around him calling out his name as she came.

He was right there with her. After a few more movements Ben stilled as he emptied himself deep inside her center.

Holy shit.

Ben gasped, trying to catch his breath as he fell next to Holly on the bed.

When his back hit one of the ornaments he let out a chuckle before sweeping his hands on the sheet making the rest of them fall off.

A small grunt came from Holly when she heard them hit the floor. "I'm telling Santa you did that."

"You think he'd believe you? I'm Head Elf after all." He winked at her.

"He better."

Ben barked out a laugh as he shook his head. "Love you, Grace."

"Love you, too, *Head Elf.*"

Holly's hand went to Ben's chest, before flicking his left

nipple. And as that same hand then migrated down to his abs, the corner of Ben's mouth turned up. "My plans exactly. The night's young and we've got hours to explore how you plan on improving the workshop's daily toy quota."

Holly instantly pushed his chest, flipping Ben onto his back as she straddled his waist. "I'll show you a daily toy quota."

"If you keep this up, Grace, you'll be Head Elf in no time." A wicked smile appeared on Ben's lips as his hands went to her hips.

"That's my goal."

CHAPTER SEVEN

"I AM *NOT* WEARING THAT."

Holly crossed her red and green striped arms over her chest as she tapped her foot on the floor, making the bell chime. She was already two seconds from having a major headache and her father was about to put her over the top. "Yes, you are, Dad."

Holly foolishly thought since Ben had taken so strongly to the costumes that maybe it'd be an easy picture to capture. Then she could actually get this Christmas card out in time and prove Mildred wrong.

Because after her talk with Ben, that was her only goal now.

Holly *had* to prove Mildred wrong.

Okay, if she was being honest, there was a part of her that still wanted to make sure everything went smoothly for the holidays. But to see the look on Mildred's face after she *did* get the cards out on time was numero uno on the list.

That old coot had won way too many arguments over the years and it was about time Holly finally won one.

"You are out of your mind if you think I'm getting in that." Henry sneered at the outfit disgusted.

"Dad, get in the dang costume. You only have to be in it until we get the picture."

"I ain't letting you have evidence of me in that thing." Henry shook his head. "No freaking way."

"Grandpa, it could be fun!" Jimmy grabbed his elf outfit holding it up in the air. "We'll all look the same."

It turned out Jimmy was a lot more like Ben than Holly thought. When the package arrived while they were adding the finishing touches to the Christmas tree Monday night, Holly had come clean and told Jimmy what she'd done.

To her complete surprise, the kid was all for it.

He remarked how neat it would be to dress up like the elves he saw when they went to see Santa at their local mall. Jimmy even went as far as to mention he should send the picture to Santa himself and see if he wanted to hire him for next year. Since he already would have the outfit after all.

Go figure.

Holly and Ben had both looked at each other dumbfounded before laughing. Holly should've known by now nothing ever happened the way she planned it.

"There ain't no fun in dressing up like an idiot."

Okay well, maybe. Her dad seemed to be pretty annoyed with the idea. "You are wearing it for the card and that's final." Holly's arm snapped to her waist, making her green puffy skirt flare out.

"I can't take you seriously when you look like that."

"I look adorable."

"You look like Christmas threw up."

Holly huffed as she took her dad's outfit and tossed it at his head. "Put it on. I'm your daughter. I don't ask for much."

His good brow shot up. "You ask a lot."

"I do not." She glared at him. "Now, put it on."

"You're pretty demanding for someone who doesn't ask a lot."

"Dad, put on the damn outfit. We are making this card. Get over it." *Why is he being so difficult? Yeah, I originally bought them to annoy everyone, but now it was more than that.*

"I ain't."

"You are."

"And why the hell is he here? Didn't I get enough of him over the weekend?" Henry jerked his head toward John who was on the couch laughing his ass off.

"I needed someone to take our photo." Holly crossed her arms over her chest again, narrowing her eyes at her father.

"And you picked him?"

"He was the easiest. Now, come on, we don't have all night. Put that damn costume on or I'll force you to wear it."

"I'd like to see you try."

"This is the best holiday ever." John burst into more uncontrollable hysterics causing Holly to snap her head to him.

"There is one in there for you too, buddy. Don't make me get it out." Her eyes hardened at John. Her headache was for sure making itself known now.

John instantly stopped laughing.

That's right, buddy.

However, before he could protest, Ben walked into the living room, making Holly's jaw hit the floor.

"I look good, don't I?"

Holy shit, Head Elf indeed. Holly swallowed hard as she looked him up and down. How the hell he was pulling this

66

off, she had no idea. Holly was absolutely sure of one thing, though. As soon as they could, they'd be dragging these out again for a replay of the other night.

Ben caught her eye before giving her the once-over. It was like he could read her mind as his eyes heated. She did think she looked rather cute in her decked-out costume.

"You look like an elf," Henry grumbled at Ben shaking his head.

"A sexy elf." He winked at Holly. "I'd have *all* the lady elves after me."

"No, you wouldn't." John jumped up from the couch.

"Yes, I would." Ben flicked the top of his ear. "I'd drive them wild."

Something flashed on John's face. "Not as much as *I'd* drive them wild."

Holly rolled her eyes as it began. Why was it always a competition between the two of them?

"Holly said she got me one too, I'm gonna put mine on and we'll see who looks better." John reached for one of the other outfits staring Ben down.

"Oh no you don't." Holly stopped John. "You two can play *after* the picture."

"But I wanna show him what an idiot he looks like and how *I'd* look ten times better," John cried.

"You wish. I look fine as hell." Ben winked at Holly once more causing her headache to turn into a full-blown migraine.

With an annoyed scoff, John puffed his chest out. "You know what, you're lucky. Your wife just stopped your ass from being slaughtered."

"No, my wife just stopped you from looking like a fool."

"You're all fools. Especially in that outfit," Henry mumbled. "I am not getting into that *thing*."

"Yes, you are." Holly swung her attention back to her father.

"No, I'm not."

Before Holly could say another word, Jimmy ran into the living room. "Look at me! Look at me!"

After Holly sent another death glare at her father, she turned to her son. *Aww, holy crapolie.*

As Jimmy stood next to Ben, her heart did a flip. They were identical down to the bells on their toes. Holly's heart warmed. Damn, screw Mildred. She was doing this for herself again. This picture was going up everywhere she could hang it. They really were going to be perfect Santa's little helpers.

Holly's eyes darted to her father again. That is if she could get him to stop bitching and just put on the damn thing.

"Ripley likes her costume too." Jimmy bounced on his feet making the bells jingle on his toes. "She let me put it on her."

Ripley trotted into the room showing off her lady elf costume. She even did a twirl making sure everyone got a good look at her fluffy skirt.

Holly couldn't help but laugh as Ripley shook her tail making the bells on the skirt jingle louder. She was definitely cute as all get out. She even had on the matching hat that had pointed ears attached to it.

See, this was going to be the best Christmas card ever.

Holly: one.

Everyone else in the world, including Mildred: zero.

Holly dropped to her knees as Ripley ran over to her. "Who's mommy's little girl? You're so pretty, Rip. Look at you." She scratched her back making Ripley jingle the bells again as she danced. The dog then kissed Holly before barking in agreement.

"You know it too." Holly nuzzled Ripley's neck. "Now, where are your brothers?"

A toothy grin appeared on Jimmy's face as he spoke up, "They're hiding under your bed."

"Of course they are." Holly flicked her eyes up at the ceiling.

Henry made another annoyed noise in the corner, causing Holly's attention to jump to him.

That's it.

A person could only take so much.

"Put on the damn outfit or I'll make you food and shove it down your throat."

"You wouldn't?"

"Try me. If I don't have this photo uploaded to the site by midnight, we won't get the cards back in time." Holly narrowed her eyes on her father, daring him to defy her. "At this point, it's about pride."

"That's not my problem," he squared off with his daughter.

"It *will* be." Holly shifted to Ben. "Get Peanut all dressed. I'll be right back with the devil and his jester."

Ben winked. "Sure thing."

As Holly stomped out of the room, her elf feet jingled as she walked. She couldn't help but curse herself as she still heard her father complaining and John laughing his ass off.

Why couldn't things ever just be normal for once in her life?

Holly eyed the ceiling. *Don't answer that, Universe. I already know I'm here for your entertainment.*

When Holly turned into her bedroom, she saw Waffles' fluffy butt hanging halfway out from under their bed. "You know I can still see you, right? You aren't invisible if you're only hiding your head," Holly groaned before looking to the ceiling again. *Really, Universe?*

Waffles barked as he tried to squash his fat butt further under the bed.

"I can still see you." Holly tapped her foot, causing the bell to jingle again.

Waffles barked at her.

"Do not speak to me in that tone of voice, young man. I don't get it. You wore your tux fine when your dad and I got married. Now, you see clothes and you run for the hills. What the hell happened? Is your old age creeping up on you? Why do you have to be so grumpy?"

Waffles grunted from under the bed.

"You will come out here right now, put this stupid costume on and have your picture taken." She crossed her arms over her chest. "Stop arguing with me."

Waffles turned so Holly could see his side profile under the bed. She growled the moment she saw that little jerk was glaring at her.

"Get your butt out here now!"

He huffed turning back so Holly couldn't see his face.

"Do *not* make me get you."

Waffles kicked his foot out toward her. "Did you just try to kick me?"

The jerk did it again.

"That's it." Holly dropped to her knees before reaching for her dog. Before she could grab him, though, the asshole managed to wiggle his way out from under the bed. And now it was a game for him as he ran back and forth trying to avoid Holly.

"Stop moving." She reached for him again only for Waffles to psych her out and run the other way.

"You're wearing the elf costume. End. Of. Story."

Waffles stopped dead in his tracks as he glared at her before barking.

When Holly took a step toward him, that damn dog turned his nose up and ran full speed at her.

"No, you don't." When Waffles ran through her legs, Holly quickly snapped them shut effectively trapping the Corgi. "There! Gotcha now."

When Holly scooped him into her arms, the jerk got his claw stuck on her stocking tearing a hole in it. "Really? I planned on reusing these."

Waffles had the gall to stare her down like that was what she deserved. "I'll remember this. You used to love wearing clothes. Then all of a sudden, boom. You were too good for them. What the hell happened? Don't you remember the wedding? You were so freaking adorable. I wanted to eat you up."

Waffles barked again giving her the side-eye.

Out of nowhere, a realization dawned on Holly. "Oh my God, are you fighting this because I mentioned you looked dashing in your wedding tux and you'd never hurt a fly?"

Waffles glared at her.

"You have got to be freaking kidding me."

He scoffed, letting out a single bark as he nodded.

"Fine, I take it back. You looked like a secret agent in that outfit. No one would've dared to take you on." It took everything inside of her not to roll her eyes.

Waffles scowled at her for one more second before he took a step closer to her, turning his nose up to the dog outfit at the end of the bed.

"Really? Fucking really?" Holly gritted her teeth as she snatched the outfit into her hands. "This is why you've been an ass? All 'cause I said you weren't intimidating enough in your outfit? I swear to everything, Waffles, one of these days I'm gonna murder you."

The dog grunted causing Holly to hold up her hands in surrender. "Kidding. I still get chills when I think of you in that outfit. *Scaryyyy.*"

Waffles turned his nose up once more before the asshole willingly let Holly put the outfit on him.

This holiday was going to be the death of her.

Once he was dressed, Waffles gave Holly another side-eye before letting out another grunt.

"You look handsome."

The dog's eyes narrowed on her as his body went full dead weight onto the bed.

"Dramatic much? I *can* say you look handsome without you thinking you aren't intimidating."

Waffles snorted.

"I did not go through all this trouble just for you to play dead. And news flash, you aren't intimidating to anyone."

Waffles gave her another evil look daring her to say it again.

"Forget it. Twitch, where are you?"

Twitch jumped onto the end of the bed, bobbing his head from side-to-side.

"Do *not* give me as much trouble as he did." She pointed at the dog still playing dead on the bed.

Twitch glanced from Waffles to Holly before walking over to his mother purring. Holly took that as a sign and carefully put him in his outfit. Once Twitch was dressed, she turned to Waffles. "You see how easy that was? You didn't need to make it difficult."

Waffles huffed again, before turning his head away from her.

"Oh my, however, can I stand it? Waffles, I have to take it back. You're not handsome at all. Instead, you're scary. Very *very* scary," the sarcasm poured out of her.

Waffles snapped his head back to her.

"Ahhhh!" Holly threw her hands over her eyes. "Don't look at me. I'll have nightmares for weeks."

At her words, Waffles jumped onto his feet with his tongue hanging out of his mouth as he smiled at her. *Oh for fuck's sake.*

Holly took a deep breath. *Why the hell is this my life?*

"All right, you two. Time to get this movin'." As Holly jumped off the bed Waffles and Twitch eagerly followed behind her.

When they made it back into the living room Ben smiled at her. "That sounded eventful."

Holly glared at her dramatic dog. "You have no idea."

Ben roared out a laugh as Henry walked out of the side bathroom, grumbling.

"Oh, Dad, you're adorable!"

"Can it, Pumpkin. I'm only doin' this 'cause Ben promised me he'd make me two more batches of his buffalo chicken."

"Yeah, yeah, you can have whatever you want as long as I get my picture. I don't care." Holly glanced around the room and realized that everyone was dressed up and ready. Her heart melted. They all looked positively festive and she loved every second of it. She clasped her hands together in glee as she watched Waffles strut through the room like he was some weird badass in his elf outfit. She had to hold back her laugh.

If he only knew...

"Can we just get this over with?" Henry tugged at the collar of his outfit.

Dad's not gonna like it when I tell him I'll make the buffalo chicken instead of Ben. She scowled at him. *Serves him right.*

"Wow," John announced. "Don't you all look jolly?" He smirked, holding up the camera. "Who is ready for this beauty?"

"Shut your face, or I'll shut it for you."

John swung his attention to Henry. "You're not a very nice elf."

"Is it nice if I stick my boot up your butt?"

"You mean your pointy shoe with a bell on it?" John corrected, causing Henry to snarl.

"Come on people, let's get this picture," Holly announced.

Let's not add murder to the holiday memories.

Quickly, Holly arranged everyone in order before placing Waffles, Ripley, and Twitch in front of them. "We're ready."

"Say cheese."

"We all look stupid. Especially Waffles." Henry pulled at the collar of his outfit staring down at Waffles as he did.

That was the exact moment when all hell broke loose.

Waffles let out a bark as he ran around in circles trying to escape the outfit, he *thought* he looked intimidating in.

Jimmy was following behind him trying to get him to stop.

"You've got to be kidding me!" As Waffles ran past her legs Holly tried to snatch him into her arms but missed. Giving up, she snapped her eyes to John. "Please tell me you got the photo before all this happened?" She turned back to her father glaring daggers at him.

"I didn't do anything."

"Yes, you did," she spat before turning back to John. "Did you get it?"

"Oh yeah, I got it." John bit his lip to stop from laughing as he shoved the display in Holly's face. "See?"

As soon as she saw it, Holly threw her hands in the air. "Oh, for the love of all things. Are you kidding me?"

There in front of her was a picture all right. A picture that had her dad tugging his collar away from his neck. Waffles was staring at her father like he was going to kill him. Jimmy's face held a shock on it that she couldn't even describe as he jumped toward their Corgi. Then there was Ben, Peanut, Twitch, and Ripley all gazing happily at the camera.

And last but not least, there of course was Holly.

Her freaking eyes were closed and her elf hat was falling off her head. She wanted to scream. "We have to do it again."

"No can do, Grace." Ben walked behind her examining the picture.

"We are."

"Waffles says otherwise."

Holly snapped her attention to the dog, who now had the outfit halfway off his body as he continued to run around the living room. While Ripley and Twitch ran after him in some weird game.

Holly's hand jumped to her forehead trying to rub away the migraine. "We *cannot* use this. We have to redo it."

Ben pointed at the dogs again. "Waffles is chewing on it. Ripley just helped him get it off."

Holly's fist clenched at her sides as she glared at her father. "Did you really have to say that?"

"I was only speakin' the truth."

Holly threw her hands in the air. "You know what, I give up. We're using this photo. Screw it."

"That's the spirit." Ben smirked.

"Says the only human looking at the camera."

"Peanut's looking too." Ben held the baby up giving her a wink.

Holly couldn't help it as she glared at her husband as her eye began twitching. "I'm never gonna forget this."

"That's the point, Grace." Ben's smile ran from ear-to-ear. "Memories."

CHAPTER EIGHT

IT'D BEEN a week since the picture incident. And yes, that was exactly what Ben was calling it now.

The incident.

It took thirty minutes of Holly trying to convince Waffles he was in fact, an evil scary dog for him to settle down. And even then, it was touch and go.

Oh, and Ben couldn't forget how Holly yelled at everyone saying she'd be cooking all the food from now on. That had gone over *really* well.

Ben had to reassure everyone multiple times that he would never let that happen. Although, Henry was still a little worried about the buffalo chicken he'd been promised.

Maybe that was because Holly told her dad that he'd never know for sure if it was her or Ben who prepared it.

The panic on Henry's face would be something Ben would never forget. Especially when Holly warned her dad he needed to watch his back.

Ben was still laughing about it.

Besides, if you asked him, he'd say the night turned out incredible. And that photo, damn, that photo was something else and summed them up perfectly. He even planned on blowing it up and giving it to Holly as one of her Christmas gifts.

Ben smirked as his mind went to Christmas gifts. He turned on his work computer before opening the internet. Off and on, he'd been browsing a couple of lingerie shops in his spare time and he finally found a few items he wanted to buy for Holly as gifts.

Of course, with every set he liked, he added two to his cart.

A wicked smile spread across his face.

Ben knew damn well he'd be ripping them to shreds off Holly's body. When his mouse rolled over a see-through green baby doll nightie, he groaned. "I'm buying three of that one."

As Ben scanned through the online store browsing through the clothes, he found a few tops Holly would probably like as well.

Another chuckle escaped him as he thought back to their recent car ride to look at the Christmas lights around town.

They'd traveled up and down the streets singing Christmas carols as they oohed and aahed at the decorations. At one point, they'd even stopped at the local coffee shop and gotten everyone a hot chocolate.

It only took two more songs and one more street before Holly ended up spilling the contents of her drink down the front of her sweater.

Ben grinned as he clicked 'add to cart' on a top he thought she would like to hopefully replace that one.

Jimmy hadn't let her live it down. Although, he couldn't blame Jimmy because Ben was still bringing it up, too. How could he not? Holly was still annoyed she'd ruined her holiday Corgi sweater.

All in all, though, Ben was happy Holly managed to relax a bit into the season. Of course, she still had her moments trying to control everything, but she'd gotten better.

At least for the most part.

A strung-out Holly was an accident-prone Holly. And Ben had thought she was a walking disaster before.

Nope. He'd been wrong.

Last night Ben tried to count the number of *new* bruises Holly had on her body, but gave up after she flicked him off and told him to shove it.

He'd only gotten to six.

The corners of Ben's mouth turned up. Damn, he loved that woman.

After completing his purchase, Ben clicked over to his calendar. As he looked over his upcoming week, his eyes jumped to the weekend.

That's when he remembered Emma agreed to watch the kids while he and Holly finished their holiday shopping. And since Ben was headed to the store to get the food for Christmas dinner after work later, toy shopping was the only other big thing that needed to be done.

He'd been at work less than thirty minutes and he'd already received about fifty text messages from Holly reminding him of things to buy for Christmas dinner.

Ben rolled his eyes as he felt the phone in his pocket go off one more time. It's not like she'd be the one cooking anything anyway. Ignoring it, Ben turned back to his calendar seeing Emma's name again. He might or might not have also told John about Emma watching the kids. Ehh, what could he say? He was tired of them tiptoeing around each other. He couldn't stop his smile as he imagined the shocked expression on Emma's face when John would magically show up at their house.

It was the holidays after all, and he wouldn't be the Head Elf if he didn't try his hand at a little matchmaking.

Santa would be disappointed in him if he didn't.

Ben's eyes glanced at the clock on the wall in his office. He only had about five more minutes before he needed to see his first client. As he clicked on the day's schedule, he let out a laugh as he saw the pet's name. He clapped his hands together.

Up first, was one of his favorite clients.

As Ben pushed himself away from his desk he couldn't help but wonder what the little guy was wearing today. He walked out of his office greeting his staff as he made his way over to the cages to check on a few of his patients.

Most of them were pretty routine. Some were staying a few days as they recuperated from surgery. While others were there so they could be given certain medications.

And then there was the bane of his existence.

Ben strode over to the grey and black tabby cat, arching his brow at the little guy. "How you doing there, Buster?"

The cat instantly turned his nose up to Ben and whined.

"You know the drill. We talked about this yesterday. Once you go to the bathroom you can leave." Ben stuck his fingers through the cage to scratch the cat's head. "I have no idea why you're fighting this."

Buster pulled back from his hand sending him a glare before blinking at him.

"As soon as we get the samples we need for the lab, you're free to go home."

Buster stared at him, not moving. "I'm giving you a few

more hours before I have to take it myself. And neither one of us wants to do that. Trust me."

Buster's eyes widened before he twisted his head to the litter box in the cage with him.

"You're killing me here, Buster." Ben decided it was best to leave the cat alone. With a shake of his head, he made his way over to exam room one.

"Where is my favorite fashionista cat?" Ben asked, as he walked into the room greeting the hairless cat Rupert and his smiling owner Abbie.

"Hey, doc. Long time no see," Abbie replied, holding her hairless cat to her chest.

"But that's a good thing. Means your little guy here has been healthy." Ben gave Rupert the once-over. The cat was dressed from head to toe, and might he add, very festively, too.

Rupert was donned in a Christmas tree sweater that included blinking lights that went on and off to the sound of *"Jingle Bells"*. He also had on a rhinestone Christmas necklace that sparkled as Rupert moved his head from side-to-side showing it off. "Well, aren't you a handsome fella? You're definitely in the holiday spirit."

Abbie placed Rupert on the exam table who gladly took that as his cue to strut back and forth showing off his outfit.

"Very nice."

"Don't encourage him." Abbie rolled her eyes.

"It's kinda hard not to." Ben laughed, watching as the cat's sweater blinked in tune.

"Ugh. He's spoiled rotten and he knows it. He's got everyone wrapped around his hairless paw."

Ben chuckled as Rupert sent him a small nod in his direction.

"My husband, Hunter, is the worst offender. You know that jerk actually *built* Rupert a dresser?"

"That so?"

"Yeah, and now this twerp thinks Hunter hung the moon. Rupert now makes *me* put his clothes away." Abbie sent an evil eye to her cat. "Between Rupert and our newborn, Hunter can do no wrong." Abbie looked at Ben. "You know, he put up *three* trees this year? He said Rupert needed his own, and then of course, since Rupert got one, so did the baby."

Ben laughed again. "Sounds about right. Congrats on the baby by the way."

"Thanks," Abbie beamed at him as pride radiated off her. "It's a hard adjustment with her here, but it's working out."

"I hear you." Ben glanced back to the cat who was still strutting his stuff up and down the table. "Catwalk time is over, Rupert. You ready for your annual check-up?"

Rupert stopped before blinking at Ben a few times.

"I'm taking that as a yes." Ben carefully removed Rupert's decked-out Christmas necklace and turned off the blinking lights on the sweater so he could complete his examination.

As soon as the lights clicked off though, Rupert hissed, narrowing his eyes at Ben.

"I'll turn them back on as soon as I'm done."

Rupert glared at him even harder.

For fuck's sake. Maybe it's me that attracts the weird animals?

It only took a few more minutes with Rupert staring down at Ben the whole time for him to complete his examination.

After a quick round of annual shots and one more check

of his heart, Rupert was good to go. "He's in perfect health as always." Ben placed his stethoscope around his neck.

"Good to know." Abbie scratched Rupert between his ears. "And here I was yelling at your father for giving you too many treats."

Rupert turned his glare on his owner causing Abbie to narrow her eyes back at him.

Wow. Just like Holly and Waffles when they go at it. Ben shook his head with a chuckle as he clicked on Rupert's sweater. "He's a good weight right now. I would try to keep him where he's at." Ben put Rupert's necklace back on, clicking it into place. "That better?"

Rupert bumped his head into Ben's hand telling him his answer.

"Stop encouraging him. You're just as bad as Hunter."

"I can't help it." Ben's smile went from ear-to-ear as he winked at the cat. "He knows how to dress."

Rupert agreed as he did another strut up and down the table showing off.

"I'll see you both next year unless something pops up. And Rupert keep looking your best self."

Rupert nodded at him, agreeing while Abbie put him back in his carrier. "Thanks, doc. See ya next year. Happy holidays."

"Same to you, Abbie."

"Thanks."

Ben gave them both a quick wave as he left the room.

"Buster *finally* went," Ben's vet tech announced, as she held up the bag. "I'm getting everything ready to ship out to the lab right now."

"Thank God. I did not want to do an extraction today." Ben glanced over at the cages, catching Buster's eyes. "It was better for both of us this way. You did great."

Buster plopped onto his side in a dramatic show causing Ben to flick his eyes to the ceiling. *It's definitely me that attracts them. Forget it.*

Just as Ben took a step toward exam room two, he felt his phone vibrate. As he rolled his eyes Ben took it out of his pocket.

Don't forget the cranberry sauce. You know, the one that's shaped like the can. We have to have that one.

Ben shook his head as he quickly sent back a text with a smile on his face. *I was thinking of trying my hand at making my own this year.*

Instantly he got a reply.

No, it has to be shaped like a can!

Of course, he was going to get the right cranberry sauce. Ben smirked as he sent back his reply. Might as well have some fun with it.

That is no way to talk to the Head Elf. You keep racking up those points there, Grace. By the way, if you're so concerned about something shaped like a can.... I'll show you that tonight.

Ben chuckled as his smile went from ear-to-ear as he headed toward the next room. When he felt his phone going off in his pocket, he knew he'd won.

CHAPTER NINE

Before Holly knew it, the week had flown by. Emma was at the house watching Jimmy and the baby while she and Ben were browsing through the store getting last-minute gifts for everyone.

So far, everyone was pretty much taken care of. However, Holly couldn't help taking one last gander through the toy aisle to see if anything would catch her eye for Jimmy.

You couldn't go wrong with getting extra gifts, right?

Plus, Jimmy deserved them.

Holly studied her notepad one more time, double and triple-checking that everyone had at least one checkmark by their name. "Okay, I think we've got everything we need."

"That's great, Grace," Ben purred, pulling her to his side for a quick kiss before letting her go.

"At least I think so." Holly's face scrunched as she squinted at him. "You got all the food stuff we need, right? And the cranberry sauce, the *canned* one?"

Ben gave her an all-knowing look. "Holly..." he warned.

"What? I'm being serious here."

Ben cocked his brow. "So am I. You know damn well I got everything. *And* if you recall, we took care of the canned cranberry sauce saga already." He sent her a wink.

"I'm just checking, gosh."

"And I'm just telling you."

"Ben…"

"Don't Ben me." Ben stopped pushing the cart. "Don't go stressing out again, Grace. You're gonna end up running into a wall."

Holly decided to ignore him as she looked at her pad again and kept walking. "No, I won't."

Just as Holly was about to run into a Christmas display, Ben grabbed her arm yanking her away from the disaster. "You were saying?"

A small growl escaped her before Holly turned her glare on the display like it was its fault. When she thought she'd gotten her point across she turned back to her husband. "I was saying you're a jerk. Now, you're positive you've got everything right?"

Ben let out a heavy sigh. "Yes, baby, I got everything we need to cook Christmas dinner."

As Holly watched her husband stroll through the aisle, she bit her bottom lip.

Now or never, Hol. Do it. He already agreed.

She took a deep breath as she gave him the best puppy dog expression she could muster, and spoke, "What do I get to help with?"

Both of Ben's brows shot to the ceiling as she stopped moving. "Nothing."

Holly crossed her arms over her chest. "What do you mean nothing? I thought we agreed I get to help. Remember when we were at my dad's for dinner? You *both* agreed I could help. I heard you with my own two ears."

"We weren't talking about you cooking, Grace."

"Well, *I* was." Her lips thinned. *Damn it! I want to help.*

"And *we* were talking about you entertaining everyone *not* being in the kitchen."

"Ben Richman, I want to contribute."

"With burn marks?" He stared her down causing her to growl again.

"You can make the salad."

"The salad?" Holly threw her hand over her chest like he'd shot her. "How could you? That's the most boring part. Come on, give me something good to make. Please, I promise I'll be super careful about it. You can even supervise me the whole time. I'll listen to every word you say."

Ben scratched the scruff on his chin. "Me being Master Chef and you as my Sous Chef could be fun. Might have to add that to our bedroom games."

"Ben, come on..."

As Ben continued through the toy aisle, he picked something up to show her. "What do you think about this race car? We might be able to kill two birds with one stone and buy one for John too? That way they can race them."

"Do not change the subject on me. I'm being serious, Ben."

"So am I." He showed both of them to her. "Do you think Jimmy would want the green one or the red one?"

"Green."

"Okay, then John gets the red one." Ben tossed both of them into the cart before picking up a silver one. "You think we should get one for Henry too?"

"Ben, I'm talking here." Holly tapped her foot on the floor.

"And, I'm trying to buy gifts for our family." He tossed the silver one into the cart as well.

"No, you're ignoring me. Come on, Ben, I just want *one* thing to contribute, as well. Please? Plus, I really do want to make up for the Thanksgiving fiasco. This would be the best present you could ever give me."

After a few moments of staring at her, Ben sighed. "If it would really make you happy, fine. Emma is bringing the green bean casserole and the sweet potatoes." He cocked his brow at her. "You think you can handle the mashed potatoes?"

Holly's whole face brightened in excitement. "Hell yeah, I can."

"Without hurting yourself?" Ben crossed his arms over his chest as his brows pulled together.

"Yes, *without hurting myself*," she mocked. "How hard could it be?"

As Ben stared at her, Holly could see his apprehension. Okay fine, she couldn't really blame him with her track record, but she could handle this.

Plus, if they turned out good, then she'd finally get to tell everyone *she* made something that didn't have any one calling the fire department or poison control.

"You have to peel them, cut them, boil them, *and* then mash them together. That's a lot of steps, Grace."

"Peel. Cut. Boil. Mash. Got it."

"Holly..." he warned, cocking his brow.

"What? I said I got it." *Geez, it's not like I'm was asking him to help me hide a body. All I want to do is cook some of the food for Christmas.*

Ben shook his head. "On second thought, maybe I should do the potatoes and you can butter the rolls."

"Butter the rolls! That's worse than the salad. At least with the salad, I get to use a knife."

"Who said you'd use a knife? I planned on getting you bagged salad that you'd just have to dump in the bowl."

Holly's lips thinned as she stared down her husband. "You wouldn't."

Ben cocked his head to the side which made Holly throw her hands up. "Nope, you already agreed I can do the potatoes. It's done and over with. That's what I'm doing. No take-backs." She stuck her tongue out at him.

Take that!

Holly: one.

Ben: zero.

"Fine." Ben quickly turned their cart around shaking his head as he walked out of the aisle and toward the other end of the store, causing Holly to run after him.

"Hey, where are you going?"

Ben walked faster as he headed toward his target. "I'm gonna buy another first aid kit. Maybe two."

Holly froze as her jaw dropped. "You asshole."

CHAPTER TEN

CHRISTMAS EVE.

How in the world was it already *Christmas Eve?* Holly looked around their living room still in awe. Where in the hell had the time gone?

One second it was Thanksgiving and the fire department was there, and then boom, it was Christmas Eve.

Just like that.

Wow.

Holly's eyes moved to their living room window. It was already dark out and in less than a few hours it would be Christmas day.

Their first Christmas together as a family. Hell yes!

Holly sat back as the memory of the evening washed over her. It ended up being pretty amazing if you asked her. Jimmy and Ben had spent a few hours making cookies for Santa while she watched.

Holly was only allowed to decorate them, though. A small grunt escaped her. The jerks.

But she showed them. Kind of. When some of the cookies were baking, a few had expanded. And it just so happened that one of those expanded cookies was a Corgi.

Of course, Holly took full advantage of it and made that cookie into an overstuffed Waffles. Would you expect anything less from her?

Nope.

Waffles wasn't a fan, though. When she showed him the cookie, he scoffed before turning his nose up at her and waddled out of the kitchen like she'd offended him.

One point for Holly.

She thought it was hilarious and so did Jimmy. In fact, he loved that cookie so much he wanted Santa to have it.

Waffles still wasn't pleased, but oh well. Maybe he'd be less of a diva going forward...

Probably not.

Once the cookies were set out for Santa, the whole family sat on the couch as they watched a Christmas movie. When it was over, Holly and Ben had tucked both of their kids into bed and read them a holiday story. Holly laughed at Jimmy tossing the covers over his head the moment the story was done. He'd even faked a few snores in there.

If it'd been up to Jimmy, he would've gone to bed sometime in the early afternoon. He kept mentioning how he'd been worried that Santa might pass over their house if he wasn't asleep yet. He even went on and on to Helen about it as she happily smiled up at her big brother with twinkling eyes, gurgling.

Which was fine by her, that girl loved to sleep.

Holly glanced back out of the window, seeing the holiday decorations outside. It really did look like something right out of a postcard. If Jimmy hadn't been asleep for the last few hours, she would've shown him how beautiful it was.

This really was turning out to be a spectacular Christmas.

As Holly's eyes drifted to the stacks of wrapped presents under the tree, a huge smile spread across her face. What could she say? She might have gone a little overboard but, hey, it was the holidays after all.

"I didn't realize we bought this much." Ben finished wrapping another gift before placing it on a pile to his right.

The soft glow from the lights on the tree illuminated Holly's face as she smiled at her husband. "It's okay. They deserve it."

Ben cocked his brow at her. "You do know we ended up buying John a crap ton of toys, right?"

Holly's eyes scanned the room looking at everyone's pile. Damn, there were a lot there for John. She rolled her eyes. She did say it was the holidays after all, and she needed to stick with it. "I guess he deserves it too. Plus, it's easy to buy for him. You just have to think of him as an eight-year-old boy."

Ben barked out a laugh as he plopped back onto the couch after moving another present under the tree. "You're right. And it will keep him and Jimmy both occupied."

"True." Holly smiled sweetly at her husband as he reached for another gift to start wrapping.

See, everything was working out just fine. As Holly sat back on the couch, her eyes caught the clock in the room, causing her to swallow hard. It was getting pretty late, and if she didn't start now it wasn't going to happen...

Was she really going to do this? Holly took a deep breath. Yeah, she was.

The idea popped into Holly's head after working a few extra shifts with Mildred. All the old coot could do was go on and on about couples using this time of year for inspiration in the bedroom.

Not that her and Ben needed any inspiration in that department. They'd been playing out the Head Elf thing quite a lot...

But then again, *that* was the reason why Holly came up with Ben's Christmas gift. Somewhere along the line, as Mildred encouraged her, Holly decided she would wrap *herself* up in a huge red ribbon and let Ben unwrap her as his gift.

She even bought one of those huge bows to go with it.

As she watched Ben wrap another gift, she bit her bottom lip knowing the ribbon and bow were in the bottom of her closet just waiting...

She could do this.

Holly even watched a couple of videos on the internet on the best way to wrap herself. You really could find anything online if you searched hard enough.

And from the tutorials Holly watched, it didn't seem *all that* complicated. Plus, she *really* wanted to see Ben's reaction.

As she sat back on the couch she closed her eyes. She could picture it in her mind. If she did it right, all he'd have to do was pull one end of the ribbon and poof, she'd unravel in front of him.

He'd love it, and so would she.

See, she could totally do this.

Ben finished wrapping another gift and leaned back on the couch with a heavy sigh. "I don't know if these gifts will ever end."

"They will."

"Only if you help." He cocked his brow at her. "You haven't wrapped anything in twenty minutes."

"That's 'cause I was thinking."

The corner of Ben's lip turned up. "I don't see any smoke."

"Jerk."

"Love you, Grace." Ben tenderly pulled Holly to him, giving her a kiss.

"Love you too. And if you *must* know, I was thinking about something for you. I've got something special planned."

That got Ben's attention. "Oh, yeah, and what's that?"

A mischievous smile appeared on Holly's face as she stood. "Meet me in the bedroom in twenty minutes." She looked around the room. "That'll give you enough time to finish wrapping and get everything under the tree."

As Ben scanned her body up and down his eyes filled with lust. "Yes ma'am." He grabbed another gift by his foot before hurrying to wrap it.

That's one way to get him to go faster and for me not to have to wrap anymore. The stupid tape was the devil. Bastard tape. I think I still have some stuck on me.

Holly laughed as she made her way down the hall to their room. Ben would be done in no time if he kept going at that rate. Holly decided it was best if she got a move on herself as she bounced into her room before shutting the door. Quickly she went over to the closet and pulled out the extra-large bow and ribbon. As she tossed the bow on the bed, she found the end of the ribbon that she needed.

"Okay, all the videos said you need to start covering your chest and then wrapping it around you, so you can tuck the end in." Holly definitely wanted to do the tucking option rather than the tape. The tape option would end really bad, knowing her. Plus, the tape had already made her its bitch a couple of times while they were wrapping the gifts.

Then again, so could this option.

Holly took another deep breath before she ripped off her clothes and started the process. She went slow and precise as she did her best to recall the videos. "Okay, now through the legs and up and over my hip and then once more on the other side, but this time I've got to—"

Her thought was cut short as Holly somehow found herself falling through the air.

CHAPTER ELEVEN

For fuck's sake.

At the sound of the crash, Ben sprinted like a bat out of hell toward the noise. He already knew whatever happened wasn't good.

And, he was right.

The moment Ben turned the corner into their bedroom, he saw a naked Holly on the floor tangled from head to toe in a red ribbon, punching the air. His eyes nearly popped out of his head as he watched her flailing around on the floor like she was fighting off an invisible attacker.

Or, you know, the ribbon.

That wasn't all of it, though.

Nope, Waffles was also on the foot of the bed chewing on one of the biggest bows Ben had ever seen.

"What the hell, Grace?" Ben shut their door as he stepped inside, making sure not to wake their kids before running over to the mess that was Holly.

"No, I wasn't ready! Get out."

"Wasn't ready for what?" Ben picked Holly up in one

swift move and sat her on the bed, doing his best to untangle her as he went.

"You're ruining the surprise."

"I'm pretty surprised all right." Ben cocked his brow, as he looked down at the woman desperately trying to untangle herself from the mess she was in. Come to think of it, he was pretty sure Holly was only making it worse. "Are you hurt?" he asked, scrutinizing her to see if there were any signs of an injury.

"My ego."

"Grace."

"Don't Grace me!" she snapped, as she tried once more to untangle herself but failed.

It took everything inside of Ben not to laugh. How could you blame him though? There he was, placing the last presents under the tree, only to hear the telltale sign of Holly once again falling somewhere in the house.

Then to be greeted the way he was? Although, he had to admit, Holly did look downright adorable. She reminded him of an angry little elf, who'd failed the wrapping portion of Santa's workshop.

An ear-to-ear grin appeared on his face as he realized he could use this to his advantage. Damn, he loved this woman.

"This is what I get for trying to seduce you," Holly grumbled. "I'm blaming Mildred for this. If she didn't get that stupid idea of *inspiration* stuck into my head in the first place, none of this would've happened."

"What idea from Mildred?"

"I was trying to wrap *myself* up as a gift and give it to you," she spat as she tugged at her arm trying to untangle it.

Ben's body instantly heated at her words as he eyed her up and down. "That's kinda hot."

"Shut up."

This time Ben did laugh. "Baby, you should know by now you never need to seduce me. I'm a sure thing."

He winked at Holly which caused a growl to escape her lips as she flailed her arms around while she still tried to untangle herself from the mess. "I'll show you a sure thing."

This should be fun to watch. Ben crossed his arms as he waited for Holly to finish thrashing around.

Holly gave up after getting nowhere, slumping into a pile of naked Holly and ribbon on the bed. "I'm pretty sure this thing is cutting off the circulation to my right boob. It's also giving me a major wedgie."

Ben barked out a laugh as he found the end of the ribbon and started untangling her. "Grace, oh, Grace. What am I ever going to do with you?"

"Leave me to my misery."

"With or without the ribbon on?" He smirked, provoking Holly to growl again.

As carefully as he could, Ben slowly worked the ribbon off Holly, before tossing it on the floor causing an eager Waffles to run after it. "Are you hurt anywhere?" he asked, examining every part of her body. The moment Ben reached her left ankle, Holly grunted. "Answer me."

Holly narrowed her eyes on him, as she replied, "I've felt worse."

"I know, but how does this feel?" He lightly squeezed her ankle.

Exasperated she gave up again as she sighed. "Not that bad, it's just a little sore. I think the ribbon got wrapped around it when I fell and landed on it. Or who the hell knows?"

Ben shook his head, carefully putting her foot down before walking into their bathroom. After he found what he was looking for, he walked back into their room. "I'm glad I got the extra first aid kit." He smirked her way. "Nothing feels broken. If it isn't better by morning, I'll drive you over to the clinic and do an x-ray."

"The hell you will." Holly crossed her arms over her naked chest as she scowled at the first aid kit. "I take it back. This is *your* fault, not Mildred's. If you hadn't bought that stupid thing none of this would've happened. You cursed me to get hurt."

It was only a matter of time. Ben's brows shot to the ceiling as he stared at his grumpy wife.

"Don't look at me like that."

"Like what?"

"Like you knew I was eventually gonna get hurt."

"Well, it is you."

"You got a death wish?"

"Those are some fightin' words from the only person that's naked in this room." Leave it to Holly to forget that detail.

"I'll use that to my advantage."

"Are you gonna attack me with your pussy?" His whole face lit. "On second thought, I'm good with that."

"Ben..." she groaned.

After scanning her up and down again, he decided it was better to make sure Holly was okay. Before they went any further, Ben dropped to his knees in front of her. "Let me take a look."

As Holly grumbled above him, he rechecked her ankle. It really did appear to be fine, only a tad red. It was more than likely just a bruise and Holly would be fine by morning.

"But I was supposed to take care of *you*. I was gonna be your present," Holly pouted, recrossing her arms over her chest.

"You're always my present."

"Ugh." Holly flung herself back onto the bed as Ben wrapped her ankle. "The videos made it seem so easy. I don't get where I screwed up."

"What videos?"

"The ones I watched on how to wrap yourself up. I had this all planned out. I was even gonna throw in a little *Head Elf* action, but no, my stupid fat body had to go and screw everything up... again."

Ben stopped what he was doing as he jumped to his feet. "Excuse me? What did you just say?"

Holly's eyes snapped toward him as panic flashed through them. "Uhhh, you look very pretty."

"That so?"

"Yes." She nodded.

"'Cause it's Christmas, I'm gonna let that slide. But you only get one pass." Ben rolled his eyes as he knelt back down to finish up Holly's ankle.

When he was done, he stood. That's when Holly groaned, kicking out her good foot to hit him but missed.

"Now, that's not very nice of you," he snickered.

"No one ever said I was nice."

"You're always nice." Ben crawled onto the bed next to his wife. "You've never once been on Santa's naughty list."

"Then why do you keep trying to report me to him?" Holly stuck her tongue out at him, causing Ben to bark out another laugh.

With a shake of his head, Ben kissed the side of her jaw. Not a day went by he didn't thank the Universe for having his frisbee hit Holly in the mouth. He had no idea how much fun life could be until Holly came along. "You're feisty when you're angry."

"Am not."

"Are too."

"I'm gonna put *you* on Santa's naughty list." The dare in Holly's eyes did something to Ben.

"Depends on what kind of naughty we're talking about?" Lust filled him as his eyes honed in on her chest.

"You're just as bad as Mildred."

"I take that as a compliment."

"You would." Holly dramatically tossed her head to the other side away from him. "I ruined our night."

"No, you didn't." Ben pushed himself onto his elbow, before kissing her cheek. "I still got to unwrap my gift, didn't I?"

"Not the way you were supposed to." Holly snapped her head back to him.

"The way I look at it, I got to be the hero and save the helpless little elf as she rolled around on the floor naked. *Then* I even got to unwrap her. I say this is a win-win. Best damn gift I've ever gotten."

"Stop enjoying this."

"Why? You're lying naked next to me. Only thing better would be if *I* was naked. Actually... let's change that." Ben jumped from the bed and removed his shirt and pants standing there in front of Holly in nothing but his Corgi Christmas boxers.

"Oh my God, where did you get those?"

"Online." He smiled at her. "You'd be amazed at what you can find there."

"Trust me, I know." Holly ignored him as she sat up staring at the Corgi in the Christmas hat, sleeping on a pillow surrounded by presents. "They are the cutest thing I've ever seen."

"I was going for sexy, but I'll take cute." He chuckled.

Just as Ben was about to remove them, he saw Holly's

eyes look past his body. Instantly her face hardened. "Do you know how much that stupid bow cost me?" she growled. "Stop chewing on it, Waffles."

Ben swung his head around, for him only to see Waffles chewing on the bow as he'd tangled himself in the same ribbon Holly had just been in.

Like mother, like son.

Ben scanned Waffles once more, making sure the ribbon wasn't hurting him and that he could get out if he wanted, before turning back to his wife. "Let him have his fun, Grace. It is Christmas after all." Ben quickly pushed down his boxers and crawled back onto the bed. "Now, it's time for some fun of our own." He kissed up her body as his hand carefully went to her left ankle cautiously looking into her eyes. "You sure your ankle's okay?"

"Trust me, I'm accident-proof."

"You and I both know that's not true."

"Fine." She rolled her eyes. "But, I'm okay. I had the amazing Doctor Richman wrap it up for me. I don't even feel a thing."

He cocked his brow at her. "I can't tell if that's sarcasm or the truth?"

"Truth. I'm pretty sure my body's used to things like this by now."

"You're probably right." He let out a laugh as he gently grabbed Holly's hips, repositioning her on the bed.

"Hey!"

"As Head Elf, and as long as you really aren't hurting, I plan on accepting my gift."

"Ben..."

Both his eyebrows shot up. "Head Elf," he corrected.

Holly flicked her eyes to the ceiling as Ben grabbed a

pillow and placed it under her hips. "Master Head Elf," she mocked. "Don't you think the mood is ruined?"

Ben tapped his finger on his chin. "Master... I can get used to that."

"Oh geez, why did I say that?" Holly threw her arm over her eyes.

"Shh, let me live out this fantasy," he remarked, moving himself between her legs. "And the mood is not ruined. It's Christmas. It's the happiest time of the year."

"Not for sexy times."

"Always for sexy times." Ben kissed the inside of her thigh. "Right now, I'm going to show you just how good Christmastime can feel."

Holly's eyes widened as she frowned at him. "No, this was supposed to be about *you,* not me."

Ben cocked his brow as he playfully nipped the inside of her thigh causing her to yip. "Wasn't this my present?"

"Yeah, but..."

"No buts, if it's my present then I get to decide how I want to use it. And right now, I want nothing more than to stick my tongue deep inside of my wife." At her shocked face, Ben winked. "Maybe the extra endorphins can help heal your ankle faster."

She flicked her eyes to the ceiling. "I feel fine right now," she protested.

"And you're about to feel a whole lot better." Ben smirked, moving himself to her core.

God, no matter how many times he'd done this, he couldn't get enough. There was something about Holly that always had and always would drive him wild.

As his tongue flicked along her opening, he squeezed her thighs with his hands.

Ben knew without a doubt, making love to Holly was

something he'd never get tired of. As he inhaled her scent, he let his tongue seek out her clit as his fingers found her core. While he worked his fingers in and out, Holly moaned causing the sound to rocket through his body.

Fuck yes. God, he loved that sound.

As Holly moved her hips, Ben finally brought her clit into his mouth.

"Yess, please," she panted, her body tightening around him.

The moment he nipped on his treasure, Holly's whole body shook forcing Ben to hold her hips in place, so she wouldn't injure her ankle any further.

After a few moments, Holly finally came down. "That's what I like to call a Merry Christmas, Grace."

Holly laughed as she shook her head at his words. "Only you." When she looked at him with nothing but pure love in her eyes, Ben's heart squeezed.

"I love you, Holly." He crawled up the bed, positioning himself at her center.

"I love you, too," she answered, pushing her hips up forcing the tip of Ben's dick to enter her.

Ben instantly looked down at her with his brow cocked and the corner of his mouth turned up. "Why you naughty girl," he chuckled. "Maybe you do belong on Santa's naughty list."

A wicked smile appeared on Holly's face. "If it would get you to move your body, I'm good with that."

"You little shit." Ben laughed as he grabbed Holly's hips, pushing him the rest of the way in.

"Ben..."

He pulled halfway out before moving back in. "Head Elf," he corrected again, as he thrust inside of her keeping his hands on her hips so she wouldn't jostle her leg, just in case.

"Please, harder," she begged.

Who was he to deny her? As he slid in and out, he felt her walls tighten around him like a vice grip. "That's it, baby. Feel me." He knew he needed to be mindful of her ankle but with Holly moving her hips to meet him thrust for thrust he nearly lost it. "Oh, shit, Holly. Fuck."

"More."

As she met him in his movements, he reached between them seeking out her nub. As soon as he found it, he feverishly rubbed causing her walls to tighten around him harder. "Come for me, Grace. Now."

At his words, Holly shook, doing exactly that. At the sensation of her exploding, Ben couldn't help it as he followed suit releasing himself deep inside of her core. Once he was done, he collapsed onto the bed next to Holly.

Holy shit.

As Holly slowly came down from her high, Ben tucked her into his side. "Merry Christmas, Holly."

"Merry Christmas, Ben," she lazily replied as she snuggled deeper into his side. "I don't know what I did to deserve you."

"I can say the same about you." He kissed the top of her head. *"*Now, get some sleep. We'll check on your ankle in the morning, but I'm positive you'll be fine."

"I don't even feel it anymore."

"That's 'cause you just experienced two earth-shattering orgasms. Your head's not in the right place."

"Earth-shattering, you think that highly of yourself?"

She stared at him with a smirk, causing Ben to quirk his brow. "You denying it?"

"No, but you don't have to say it like that."

He laughed. "I'm only speaking the truth."

"Yeah, yeah," she remarked, casually molding her body into a more comfortable position on her side. "Hey! Don't look at us like that."

Ben glanced over Holly's body to see Waffles giving them both the most disgusted look he could muster toward them.

"You were the one that wanted to stay in here to eat the bow," Ben reminded him, causing Waffles to glance back at the destroyed bow and then back to them with another look of disgust on his face.

"That's what you get." Holly stared him down. "Next time, don't eat the gift I was using to give to your father."

Waffles turned his nose up to them and huffed his disagreement.

"Waffles. So help me God, I'll—"

"Go to sleep, Holly," Ben interrupted. "He's not worth it. Plus, before you know it, it'll be Christmas morning. Then all the fun can start."

Holly snapped her attention back to her husband, Waffles long forgotten. Her whole face glowed with an excitement Ben hadn't seen in a while. "That's right! When do you think I should start the potatoes?"

Ben flung his head back onto the pillow as a heavy sigh escaped him. "I was hoping you'd forgotten about that."

"Peel. Cut. Boil. Mash!"

We're all doomed.

CHAPTER TWELVE

CHRISTMAS MORNING

WHAT A FREAKING MORNING.

Okay, Holly's night might have also been a factor in her good mood, but dang, she couldn't help it. She was energized.

Holly was the first one up and after she checked to make sure she could put weight on her foot, she hightailed her ass out of bed and quickly donned her *Elves do it better* pajama set she'd bought last minute and jumped on top of Ben to wake him.

When his grump ass *finally* opened his eyes, Holly ran to Jimmy's bedroom doing the same to him. All the while demanding everyone got their butts out of bed and into the living room.

At first, Jimmy had thrown a stuffed animal at her head, but as soon as he realized what was going on, he shot out of bed faster than anything Holly could have imagined.

It was Christmas morning! *Duh.*

Between Holly and Jimmy, it was a race to the Christmas tree.

Of course, Jimmy won, but Holly might have let that

happen on purpose. The second she saw Jimmy's face light up as he excitedly looked all around the room, Holly knew it was her who'd really won.

Jimmy's eyes twinkled as he skidded to his knees in front of the tree examining all of the presents. "Santa came!"

"It sure looks like he did, Kiddo." Holly's smile went from ear-to-ear as her heart twisted in pure happiness. As she watched Jimmy bounce from one end of the tree to the other while he laughed, it was everything Holly could've asked for.

When Jimmy turned back to her with the biggest smile she'd ever seen on his face, everything felt right in the world.

Hearing a noise, Holly glanced over her shoulder to the hall as Ben slowly made his way into the living room with a gurgling Helen in his arms.

"Took ya long enough." She winked at him as the corner of her mouth curved up.

Ben cocked his brow at her. "It's five-forty-five in the morning."

"Yeah. And your point is?"

"Nothing." Ben shook his head with a chuckle as his eyes scanned her body from top to bottom. "Elves do it better, huh?" His voice dropped. "That would've done just as well as the ribbon."

Holly's cheeks heated as she glanced down at her top. "This was my plan B."

"It'll be your plan A tonight." He smirked with a wink.

Before Holly could reply, Ben turned to their son. "Merry Christmas, Jimmy."

"Merry Christmas, Dad!" Jimmy dropped one of the gifts he was eyeing and ran over to his baby sister, kissing her on the head. "Merry Christmas, Peanut."

"What am I, chopped liver?" Holly's brows pulled together, hiding her smile as she stared down at a grinning Jimmy.

"Not today." He threw his body with full force at Holly giving her a huge bear hug. "Merry Christmas, Mom."

"That's better." She squeezed him back as she kissed the top of his head. "Merry Christmas, sweetie."

"That sure is a crap ton of gifts," Ben remarked, nodding his head at the tree. "Looks like everyone in this house ended up on Santa's good list."

A boyish smile appeared on Jimmy's face. "Even Waffles?"

At his name, Waffles waddled his butt into the living room and plopped down on his stomach.

Holly rolled her eyes as her dog then flopped onto his side kicking out his back legs. "Yes, even Waffles, although it was touch and go there for a little while."

Waffles lifted his head off the floor staring her down.

"Don't get mad at me. I'm only speaking the truth."

Waffles snorted, then dropped his head back down, ignoring Holly.

I should've made that Corgi cookie ten times bigger just out of spite. The jerk.

The moment Twitch and Ripley came bolting into the room they froze when they saw the tree. Ripley barked as she danced in circles with Twitch trying his best to copy her.

"Good to see you're both in the spirit." Holly smiled at them before turning her glare toward the Corgi, who once again kicked his leg out to hit her. *Asshole.* "Maybe you should learn something from those two, Waffles?"

The dog rolled onto his back dismissing her.

"I guess you won't get the presents Santa left for you. I *think* he might have even left you a new bone."

At the words, Waffles jumped up. His face darted to Holly before he honed in on the Christmas tree.

Before anyone knew it, Waffles took off full speed toward the tree, bulldozing a stack of presents in his wake.

"Oh, for Pete's sake." Holly stomped her foot. "That's *not* what I meant by being in the spirit."

Waffles looked back, giving her the side-eye as he used his nose to nudge a gift out of his way. She had to hold back her growl as Waffles daringly stared her dead in the eye as he did it again.

"You're lucky it's Christmas, mister." Holly crossed her arms as a faint smile appeared on her face. *I don't know why I expect anything less at this point.* Holly let out a laugh as she looked at him.

Just to make a complete ass out of himself, Waffles left the pile and trotted her way. However, the moment Holly reached her hand down to pet him, he faked her out running back to the tree toppling over another stack of presents.

"Waffles!"

The dog then had the balls to pop his head out from under the tree, sending Holly the glare of all glares.

That's it. Waffles is what we're having for dinner.

The moment Holly took a step toward Ben, Ben grabbed her arm pulling her to his side. "Don't let him get to you. That's what he wants."

Holly snapped her eyes back to her dog. "I'm not gonna forget this."

Ben threw his head back laughing as Waffles smiled at Holly causing her to throw her hands in the air giving up. "Waffles always seems to win, Grace."

"Yeah, and that jerk freaking knows it too." After she gave up, Holly plucked Peanut from Ben's arms. "I'm gonna get the coffee ready and feed this one while you deal with that." Holly hitched her thumb over her shoulder, pointing at the two hell-hounds who were now playing a game of hide and seek in between the presents.

"Anything for you, Grace." Ben kissed her on the lips before shifting his attention to Jimmy. "Wanna help me wrangle up these guys?"

"Yeah!"

❄

An hour and a half later, and after about twelve more arguments with Waffles, Jimmy was opening his last present.

Holly's eyes looked through the room at the aftermath surrounding her, causing a ridiculously wide smile to appear on her face.

She did it.

She freaking did it!

Holly wanted to pat herself on the back.

As she sat back on the couch, Holly kicked her legs up onto the coffee table. As far as Christmas mornings could go, this was by far the best.

"Mom?"

"Yeah, baby?" Holly smiled at her son, who was studying her with his head cocked to the side.

"Why is your ankle wrapped?" Jimmy put down his remote-controlled car and crawled over to Holly's legs to examine them. "I didn't notice it until now."

Before Holly could answer, Ben chimed in. "Mom wasn't asleep when Santa came and she was forced to tackle him to the ground to stop him from seeing her." Ben smirked at Holly trying to hold in his laugh.

"You did *what*?" Jimmy's eyes practically exploded out of his head as he stared at her. "Is that why I heard a crash last night? I was gonna check but I was worried it was Santa and I didn't want him to think I wasn't asleep. I didn't know you *tried* to kill him, Mom. I would have definitely gotten out of bed to save him."

"I did *not* try to kill Santa!"

"Think of all the children in the world, Mom. You would've disappointed them all if you'd hurt him."

Holly growled as she punched Ben in the arm. "That's not what happened. You tell him. I do not need my son thinking I tried to kill Santa."

Jimmy's face turned into a playful smile. "I don't know, Mom. You've been known to resort to violence. Look how you just punched Dad in the arm."

Holly's jaw hit the floor. "How could you? And on Christmas morning nonetheless. My own son." Her hand went over her chest.

Ben burst into a hearty laugh as he held his stomach trying to control himself.

"Shut up, Ben," Holly snapped, glaring at him. "Tell him I did no such thing."

A wicked smile emerged on Ben's face as he turned to their son. "Even though, it would've been *epic* to witness... No. Sadly, Waffles pushed your mom out of bed and she landed on her ankle."

"Oh." Jimmy shrugged his shoulders, believing that was plausible and went back to playing with his toy. "Makes sense. As long as you didn't go after Santa, Mom. That would've been inexcusable. You'd be on his naughty list for life."

Holly glared at her husband as she held Peanut in her arms. "I'm gonna get you back for this."

"I'd like to see you try, Grace." Ben smiled, taking Peanut from Holly's arms. "It looks like you're ready for a nap. Who knew Christmas Morning would take so much out of you?" Ben kissed Helen's head before walking out of the living room, ignoring a glaring Holly on the couch.

"That's so funny. Mom, check out Waffles," Jimmy distracted her from her plot to seek revenge on Ben, which made Holly's attention go back to the tree.

Her eyes instantly found a fast-asleep Corgi in a pile of discarded wrapping paper with a bone hanging halfway out of his mouth.

Holly's whole face softened as she watched Waffles kick in his sleep. "Isn't that just adorable? Too bad he's not like this all the time."

Jimmy laughed again. "He's even snoring."

"He's doing it to be cute."

"Well, it's working."

"I know." Holly flicked her eyes to the ceiling. "That jerk."

Holly saw Ripley and Twitch slowly inch their way toward Waffles out of the corner of her eye. She knew exactly what was coming next. "Don't even think about it you two." Holly pointed at Ripley and Twitch who were seconds from pouncing. "For once in his life, he isn't being a butthole. Let's keep it like that."

Ripley watched Holly for a few moments before glancing back at Waffles. She saw the exact moment in Ripley's brain when she'd made her choice.

In less than a second, Ripley pulled back before jumping onto her brother with all her might. Followed by little Twitch doing the same.

"Dang it!"

Their attack scared Waffles so bad, he farted as his life flashed before his eyes.

"Eww, Waffles, that's gross." Jimmy laughed, as he waved his hands through the air.

Waffles turned to Holly like she was the one that'd betrayed him. "Don't look at me like that. I didn't jump on you. Your sister and Twitch did."

Waffles darted his scowl toward Ripley, who was now playing with Twitch in the discarded wrapping paper that was once Waffles' bed.

Oh, for fuck's sake.

"Here it comes." Holly let out a heavy sigh.

Waffles backed up, shaking his butt from side to side ready to make his move. Just as he was about to jump, Ben walked back into the room. "They got you fair and square, Waffles."

Instead of going after his sister, Waffles snapped his eyes to Ben.

"I'm sure you'll get her back eventually."

Waffles grunted loudly before sulking his butt out of the room.

"How long do you think he'll play the victim?" Ben asked, as the corner of his lips turned up into a smile.

Jimmy jumped to his feet. "Until we start cooking!"

"You're probably right." Holly watched as Waffles turned back one more time giving everyone an evil look before stomping away.

"I know I'm right," Jimmy giggled watching Waffles leave. "I know my dog."

That he did.

Holly laughed while jerking her head toward the direction Waffles went. "Go give him some pity scratches and get dressed. You and Dad need to get Grandpa before everyone starts arriving."

"Isn't he gonna know I'm only doing it 'cause he walked away upset and in a mood?"

"When is Waffles *not* in a mood?" Holly quirked her brow at him.

"True!" Jimmy chuckled. "Waffles, I'm coming! And you're the biggest scariest dog the whole world has ever seen." With that, Jimmy took off out of the room.

Holly eyed her husband, a small smile on her face as she shook her head. "At least we aren't the only ones having to deal with his highness anymore."

"Jimmy does make it easier in that department. Doesn't he?" Ben plopped onto the couch pulling Holly into his arms.

As he kissed the top of her head, she snuggled into his side. "We did good, Ben."

"That we did."

He tightened his grip around her shoulders as a wicked smile appeared on Holly's face. "Now, when do I start the potatoes?"

"Fuck!"

CHAPTER THIRTEEN

"Don't cut yourself, Grace." Ben eyed Holly with a warning. "I don't want to go to the ER today." As he studied her up and down, a smile appeared across his face. "Although, they can always check out your ankle while they are at it."

"*I don't want to go to the ER today,*" Holly mocked, glaring at him. "I'm *not* gonna cut myself. And for your information, my ankle is fine. See, I'm standing on it, aren't I?" She bounced a few times.

"For now." He laughed, giving her a look. "The moment I unwrap it, who knows what will happen."

Holly growled. "You aren't taking this away from me, Ben." She pointed the knife in his direction, causing him to hold up his hands in surrender.

"Down, killer."

Before Holly could reply, John walked around the corner into the kitchen carrying the red remote-controlled car he'd ripped open when he'd arrived. "Why does she have a knife?" He fell backward, hitting the wall dropping his toy on the ground. "Oh God, I thought you said she wasn't cooking?" John's eyes quickly shot to Ben. "Did you lie to me?"

"I—"

"Are you trying to kill us?" John interrupted, in a panic turning his angry glare back on Holly.

"Who's killing who?" Emma asked, walking into the kitchen. She and her Great Dane, Bruce, arrived shortly after John did.

"Holly's cooking," John answered, not taking his eyes off Emma as he eyed her up and down.

Ben couldn't help but laugh. Every time Emma walked into the room, John was glued to her. Hell, he didn't know how the guy managed to walk around the house without running into something.

"For real?" Emma shot her eyes to Ben. "I hate, and trust me I *hate* to agree with John but he has a point here." She cautiously glanced at Holly who was now pointing the knife at her.

"Some best friend you are," Holly snapped. "All of you can kiss my ass. Ben promised me I could make the mashed potatoes and that's exactly what I'm gonna do."

When John was finally able to tear his eyes away from Emma, he shot a death glare at Ben. "You're an idiot."

"Do *not* call my husband an idiot." Holly turned the knife toward John. "He trusts me."

John's brows shot up as he stared at his best friend, who shrugged. "I grabbed an extra first aid kit at the store and some supplies from the clinic yesterday."

John instantly flung his hands up. "This is gonna be a disaster," he groaned before turning to Emma. "What did you bring, so I know what's safe to eat?"

At his question, Emma's whole face brightened with

pride as she stood taller. "Broccoli casserole and green bean casserole."

"Vegetables, blah." John shuddered. "It'll have to do, though, or..." He glanced at Emma again as his eyes twinkled. "Wanna go out to eat?"

"Don't you dare." Holly waved the knife around through the air, causing Ben's heart to drop. *Oh shit, this was a bad idea. A very bad idea...*

"Maybe it'll be okay?" Emma shrugged, forcing a smile on her face as she anxiously glanced around the room.

"You remember Thanksgiving." John's eyebrow quirked up.

"Again, he has a point." Emma's eyes moved to the burn marks on the walls. Apologetically she shifted back to Holly, her eyes darting from the spot back to her best friend once more.

"She's *just* making the potatoes," Ben interjected. "Everything else I'm making."

John narrowed his eyes at him. "I've heard that one before."

"She's only doing the potatoes, I promise." And if Ben were lucky, he'd somehow get Emma to make them and get that freaking knife away from Holly.

Ben reached for his pocket, checking to make sure his phone was there just in case. You never knew when you'd need to dial nine-one-one when Holly was involved.

A deep growl escaped Holly as she glared at everyone in the room. "I'm making these damn potatoes, and you all are gonna sit down at the table and eat them or I will shove them down your throat."

"Holly," Ben warned.

"Don't Holly me." She pointed the knife back at him.

Yep, this was a horrible mistake.

"What's all the ruckus going on in here?" Henry walked into the kitchen and seeing what Holly was doing, he froze. "Who the hell gave her a knife?" Henry turned to Ben who let out a sigh.

"Say it ain't so?" Henry pleaded with his daughter. "Pumpkin, you aren't supposed to be in the kitchen. When Ben and I said you could help, the food was *not* what we were talkin' about."

"I'm making the freaking potatoes," Holly spat, narrowing her eyes at her father.

As Henry completely ignored his daughter, he shifted his attention back to Ben. "How'd she convince you to agree to something so stupid?"

Fuck if I know. He held in his smile. *"Well, it probably had something to do with her pussy but still.* Ben shrugged, shaking his head.

"Emma and I were just discussing going out to eat," John announced, walking over to Henry. "Wanna join us?"

"So help me God if you all don't shut up, I will shut you up myself." Holly dropped the knife on the counter, throwing her hands to her hips.

"Hurry grab the knife!" John tried reaching for it, but Holly snatched it back.

Damn. Ben sighed. *He almost had it too.*

"This is Christmas dinner. We are all gonna have a great meal, and you won't die from my cooking." Holly pursed her lips together, making Ben hold in his laugh at her attitude. She might be seconds from stabbing herself or someone else, but she was at least adorable as she did it.

"Says who?" John countered.

"Says me." Holly angrily pointed the knife toward the back door. "Now, go outside and play with Jimmy and the dogs. I'm sure they'd love to chase after the cars. Before I decide to make something else, and I'll force you to eat that too."

"Bruce might be afraid of them," Emma commented, trying to change the subject. "I don't think he's ever seen a remote-controlled car before."

Holly jutted her head toward the back door. "Ripley's out there with him and he loves her. She'll keep him safe."

"He is the biggest scaredy-cat I've ever seen." Henry laughed as a lopsided grin appeared on his face.

"Hey, he is a scaredy-*dog*, thank you very much." Emma crossed her arms over her chest. "And there is nothing wrong with him."

"Never said there was. I like him."

Emma instantly softened at Henry's words. "Good. He likes you too. Which is surprising since he hates men."

"He doesn't hate me." John puffed out his chest as he pushed his hair out of his face.

"Depends on the day."

"It's Christmas, so he can't hate me today."

When John winked at her, Emma smiled sweetly back at him. "We'll see."

Henry snapped his fingers getting John's attention. "That big old oaf never hates *me*."

At his words, John growled. "He likes me better than you."

"No, he doesn't."

"John, does everything really have to be a competition with you?" Emma asked, rolling her eyes.

"You remember the baby shower? He and Ben still argue about it," Holly replied, waving the knife in the air again.

"Can you stop doing that?" Emma pleaded. "You're freaking me out."

"She's freaking all of us out." Ben walked over to Holly grabbing the knife from her hand.

"Hey, give that back!"

"You're not even ready for it." Ben stared down at her, as Holly popped her hip out, crossing her arms over her chest.

"Thank God. I was getting worried there he was actually gonna let her cook." Henry held up his race car. "Now, let's stop this squawking and get to the good stuff." He jutted his head to John. "Bet I can beat your ass around the backyard before you can even get your car moving, punk."

"Who you calling a punk, old man?" John growled at Henry.

"You."

"Oh, yeah?"

"Yeah."

Ben grinned as the two men stared each other down. "I don't know why either of you even bother. We all know Jimmy will kick both of your asses. He's my son after all."

"And my grandson."

"I'm his favorite uncle!"

Ben smirked. "And if I were out there, I'd beat all of you."

"But, you're not." John shifted his attention back over to Henry. "I've figured it out. Benny here is too afraid he'll lose. Once again he's all talk and no game."

"Nope. You're wrong." Ben quirked his brow at his best friend. "I *know* for a fact I'd win. But would you rather want me out there kicking your ass or in here cooking?"

John's eyes widened as they shot to the angry Holly who was still pouting. "Uhhh. Shit. Okay, fine. You win this round but right after dinner we're going head-to-head."

"You're on." Ben narrowed his sights on him daring

John to say anything else.

However, before John could, the back door slammed open. "Uncle John, Grandpa Henry, come play with me! You're taking too long," Jimmy shouted, as Waffles ran inside as fast as he could before skidding out and then running out of the back door. "Waffles' got the zoomies. Come on!"

"Coming!" Henry hollered, trailing after a runaway Jimmy who raced after Waffles.

John hastily spun back to Emma. "Keep an eye on her." He pointed at Holly. "You're the only one I trust here."

"Isn't that sweet of you," Emma replied.

John's brow cocked as he gazed down at her. "If you want sweet, all you gotta do is ask, Em." As he leaned in, Emma expertly ducked under his advance before turning to Ben. "What can I help with?" she asked, nervously avoiding John's gaze.

Ben couldn't help but send an apologetic look toward John who quickly shrugged it off. He still didn't know Emma's full story, but his heart went out to her and John. Hopefully, soon enough they could work it out. As Ben decided it was best to break the tension, he sweetly smiled at Emma before nodding his head to Holly. "You can keep an eye on her." He handed Emma the knife.

"Hey..." Holly's brows pulled together. "I don't need supervision. I watched a few tutorials on how to make them already. You were sitting right there when I was doing this morning."

"Yeah, and you watched tutorials on the ribbon and look how that turned out."

"What ribbon?"

Holly darted her head to John who had his head cocked to the side. "Never you mind."

"How about I cook them with you?" Emma asked, cheerfully trying to help the situation. When Holly didn't budge, she continued, "How about I help only if you need it? That way Ben can be focused on the main dish."

Holly thought about it for a moment before nodding. "Okay, fine. But that's *my* knife."

John groaned. "Can't you just give her like two potatoes, so she can pretend she cooked the food? And after she fucks it up, it won't be a big deal 'cause we'll have more."

"I can hear you."

John grinned at Holly. "I know. I said it right in front of you."

Emma stepped in front of John placing her hand on his chest. And the moment she did, John's whole body melted into her. "Go out back and play with Jimmy and Henry. I'll make sure nothing bad happens in here. You trust me, right?"

John's face softened as he nodded his head slightly. "I'll always trust you." He then flicked his eyes to Holly pointing at her. "It's her I don't trust."

"But, you trust me." Emma pushed his chest. "Go have fun."

John leaned into her once more. "I hope one day you can learn to trust me too." Before Emma could say anything, John straightened. "If you need me, I'll be outside kicking everyone's ass." With that, John trotted out of the door leaving Emma staring at the spot he'd just vacated.

After a few awkward moments, Holly broke the silence. "You okay?"

"Uh, yeah..." Emma swallowed hard, putting the knife down onto the counter.

"You sure?" Holly asked again.

"Yeah."

Ben watched a sad expression flash through Emma's eyes before she quickly pushed it away. And as Holly sneakily reached her hand out to grab the knife again, Emma jumped in stopping her. "Why is your ankle wrapped? What did you do?"

Holly snatched her hand back like she'd been burned before darting her attention to Ben.

"Why are you glaring at me, Grace? I didn't do anything."

Holly's lips pursed together as she shifted back to Emma ignoring Ben's laugh. "I fell."

"Sounds about right." The corner of Emma's lips rose as she playfully winked at her best friend.

And just like that, all the tension was gone as Emma walked over to the potatoes that were in a bowl in front of Holly. "Okay, how about I wash them and then we can start?"

Holly's eyes went round. "Wait, you have to wash them?"

Oh, for fuck's sake. He should have said anything other than the potatoes.

Ben looked to Emma, a plea in his eyes. "You're in charge of her. Don't let her out of your sight."

Emma picked up a potato tossing it in the air before she caught it. "Got it, boss."

Lord help us.

❄

It took over thirty minutes for Holly and Emma to wash and peel all the potatoes. At this rate, Holly was going to be an old woman before she actually did anything useful, *or* fun.

Holy crap on a cracker, why are there so many potatoes?

And why are they so wet? Holly rolled her eyes. They did *not* need to wash them. They pretty much washed themselves.

When Emma got Holly's attention, she saw the fear in Emma's eyes. "We need to cut them into smaller pieces so they can cook evenly."

"Finally!" Holly reached for the knife but Emma stopped her.

"If you are so hell-bent on doing this, we have to go slow. I don't want you bleeding everywhere."

"I'm not a child."

"But you are *Holly.*"

Ben chuckled from the other side of the room.

"Shut your face, Ben." Holly ignored her husband as she shifted her attention back to Emma. "I'll be careful, I promise."

"This is how you do it." Emma took one of the peeled and washed potatoes, tucked her fingers under and cut it in half. "See, if you do it like this, even if the knife slips you shouldn't hurt yourself."

Holly watched closely as Emma finished slicing the potato. It didn't look *that* hard. And it wasn't like this was her first time using a knife. *Cutting potatoes yes, using a knife no.*

"You try, but please be careful."

Holly cautiously took the knife from her friend and did exactly what she'd been shown. Boom, just like that, one potato was tossed in the pot, cut into the perfect size. "See, I told you. I got this."

Go me!

"We'll see." Emma smiled nervously at her. "Just go slow."

And she did. Holly took each one out and carefully did

what Emma had taught her to do. One by one, she cut them before she flung them into the pot. Everything was going perfectly, until out of nowhere, Holly felt a sharp claw dig into her foot.

"Ouch." That's when it happened. "Shit! Owwie!"

Holly dropped the knife as she held her finger in her other hand. *Oh crap, oh crap, oh crap. This is it. This is my end. I'm gonna bleed to death, or worse. If I don't bleed to death, I'll never live this down. I'll never be allowed in the kitchen again! Shit!*

Holly looked at her feet only to see Twitch pulling at the wrapping on her ankle. "This is all your fault!"

Twitch raced off as Ben came running from the other side of the room. "What did you do?" He grabbed her hand.

"It was Twitch."

"Twitch didn't cut you. You cut you," he grumbled as he examined her finger.

"You were doing so well, too." Emma shook her head, while simultaneously wiping her hands on her apron. "I'll get the first aid kit."

Just as Emma walked out of the kitchen, the front door slammed open and in walked Mildred and her husband.

And to absolutely no ones surprise, Mildred had on a tacky Christmas sweater. One with Santa bent over with Mrs. Claus behind him saying, *who's on the naughty list now?*

Holly squeezed her eyes closed trying to decide what was worse. Her finger, or Mildred.

Right now, she was going with Mildred.

Kill me now.

"The fun has finally arrived!" Mildred shimmied her shoulders, causing the bells on her sweater to jingle. "Now, we can get this party started."

CHAPTER FOURTEEN

As Ben finished the last bite of his dinner, he sat back in his seat with a smile on his face and a full belly. He couldn't complain about the day, because everything turned out better than he expected.

Even the potatoes.

Ben's eyes drifted to Holly's bandaged finger as he shook his head from side to side. She was one hundred percent going to be the death of him one day.

At least today's accident was only a small cut to her finger. He was just glad it didn't need stitches. Although, he was grateful he'd grabbed those supplies from the clinic just in case. Thank God he didn't need them. Giving Holly stitches was not an easy task as he'd found out early on in their relationship.

Ben flicked his eyes to the ceiling, holding in his laugh. Holly was still blaming Twitch. Of course, there was a possibility of that, but then again this was Holly after all. The number one award winner of tripping over thin air.

At least, for the most part, the rest of the day remained accident-free. Well, he couldn't discount Holly tripping over her feet, nearly tossing the green bean casserole all over the dining room table. But all things considered, that was a typical day for them.

As long as there was no more bloodshed, things were good.

While Ben's eyes moved throughout the room, he caught a glimpse of Mildred's sweater again.

He didn't know why at first he'd been surprised with her choice of clothing. He chuckled. Sure, it was a little hard to explain to Jimmy what Mildred was wearing, but even that turned out okay. Jimmy ended up shrugging and saying something along the lines of, "That's Mildred."

And Ben honestly couldn't agree more.

Mildred's husband was a saint and Ben couldn't figure out how he did it.

At least she was fun as hell.

A pleasant sigh escaped Ben as he observed everyone sitting around the table. He couldn't help the ear-to-ear grin on his face as he sat there.

This was his family.

After his dad died, and well, disowning his mother he never imagined he'd be here, surrounded by everyone he loved. "I know we're all still eating, but I wanted to thank you for coming. It means a lot to spend these moments together as a family."

As Holly glanced at him, a soft smile formed on her face. Ben never wanted this moment to end. This is what the holidays were about. Being together.

"Thanks for inviting us, even if Holly did cook something."

Oh, for fuck's sake.

"Shut your face, Mildred." Holly snapped her attention

from Ben to the old woman, glaring at her. "The potatoes turned out yummy."

"Only 'cause Emma helped," Mildred couldn't resist retorting with a shit-eating grin on her face. "I honestly don't know why you even tried, missy? I'm disappointed we didn't get to call the fire department, though."

Holly's nostrils flared as she let out a growl.

Emma dropped her fork on her plate. "Holly did most of the work." She glanced around the room anxiously. "I only took over while Ben bandaged her up."

"And that's why we got to eat them." John sent a death glare to Ben. "I *told* you."

"Shut your face. I put the butter in *and* mashed them. Ya jerks. At least, as good as I could with this stupid thing on my finger." She waved the bandaged appendage around before turning her glare on it. "Stupid finger."

"At least you only cut yourself once, Mom."

Holly's jaw hit the floor as the bandaged finger went over her heart. "Jimmy!"

"What? You did good, Mom. I'm proud of you." His boyish smile lit up the room, causing Holly to toss her napkin at his face.

When he caught it, everyone laughed.

"You did a good job adding the butter and mashing them, Grace." Ben reached over the table, grabbing her hand in his before squeezing it.

Play it cool, Ben. If you give her this one, she'll never ask to cook again.

"Thank you." Holly lifted her chin in defiance. "I really did, didn't I?"

"No one ended up in the hospital. I say that's a win," Mildred announced with another grin on her face. "But we still have to digest the food."

"All of you can shove it. This has been a great day." Holly swung her fork at everyone as Helen burped. "See, even Peanut said so."

"Says the person with the bandaged finger? But sure, we'll go with that." Mildred shifted her attention as she pointed back and forth between Holly and Emma. "Although, it would've been a hell of a lot better if you had your men dress up in Santa outfits and give me a little show."

All the blood drained from Emma's face. "John's not my man."

"You keep telling yourself that, young lady." Mildred turned back to Holly ignoring the frazzled Emma. "I expected more out of you."

"Mildred..." Holly warned.

"Don't Mildred me. When I agreed to come here, I was promised a show." Mildred's eyes flicked to Ben, expectantly.

Ben shrugged, with a laugh. "John and I do have an elf costume?"

Holly snapped her fingers on her good hand getting Mildred's attention. "You know damn well you weren't."

"You sure?" Mildred's brows pulled together as she faced her husband. "Didn't I say she promised me a show?"

"You talk a lot, dear. I normally just agree." He winked at Holly, as he placed a fork full of food in his mouth.

Mildred leaned into her husband's side kissing his cheek. "And that's why we've been married for the past forty-eight years."

"Has it been that long?" He cocked his brow at her.

"If you want to make it forty-nine, I'd just nod your head. I know people." Mildred gave him *the* look.

"Yes, dear." He shook his head.

Turned out, this ended up being the show for Ben and he sure as hell wasn't complaining. As long as there weren't any more disasters, he'd consider today an enormous success.

❄

For fuck's sake, Mildred was going to be the death of Holly one of these days. Although, it was fun to watch Emma still squirm in her seat.

Lord knows Holly had been on the receiving end of Mildred's match-making skills far too many times to count.

Hell, the old coot *still* texted Ben whenever Holly was in a bad mood at work to *pound some sense into her*. Holly wanted to smack herself in the forehead. She still regretted giving Mildred Ben's number in case of an emergency.

Maybe I should change our cell phone numbers? Ugh, what's the use? She'd end up calling the clinic or worse.... Holly shuddered. *Officer Jones.*

As John and Mildred blathered on about the elf costume, Holly caught Ben's eye. He sent her a quick wink before turning back to the conversation to argue who looked better in the outfit.

God, she loved him. He might be a pain every once in a while, but he really did have her best interest at heart. Even if that meant not letting her in the kitchen.

She definitely lucked out in marrying Ben.

Holly glanced around the room again.

All in all, though, even with Mildred being Mildred, everything turned out really well.

However, as Holly sat back in her seat, she heard a faint rattling noise come from the other room. At first, Holly thought she'd imagined it, but then she heard it again. "Did you guys hear that?"

Everyone stopped talking as they turned to her. "Hear what?" Ben asked.

Then it happened again. "You don't hear that noise?"

"What noise, Pumpkin?" Henry asked, searching around the room just like everyone else was.

"Benny, are you sure it was only a small cut? I think she's lost too much blood and is losing it." Mildred quirked her brow at Ben.

"There it is again!" Holly jumped from her seat and headed toward the noise. The moment she peered over her father's head at the end of the table, she saw the top of their Christmas tree swaying back and forth in the living room. "What the hell?"

That wasn't all of it, though. No, not by a long shot. Not only was her tree moving, but all three of the dogs were standing on their hind legs inches from the tree examining it.

Even Bruce was toe-to-toe with Waffles sniffing around. That surprised her, Holly could have sworn at the first sign of anything unusual, Bruce would have taken off running and ended up halfway under the bed or something like that.

Guess she was wrong.

As Bruce pushed himself higher in the air, almost reaching the top of the tree, Holly's heart stopped. "Get down. You're gonna knock over the tree!"

Holly should've known better. The moment the words were out of her mouth, Bruce panicked falling face-first into the tree.

It all happened in the blink of an eye. One second the tree was up in all its glory. The next it was on the ground as Waffles and Ripley barked and jumped on top of it.

"What the crap? Stop it you dumb-dumbs." Holly ran into the living room, stopping in front of the toppled-over mess, only to see Twitch poke his head out of the branches bobbing his head from side-to-side. "Oh my God. Was this your fault?" Holly yelled, glaring at her cat as her heart raced.

I should murder all of you.

Twitch blinked at her as the three dogs ran around the room in complete chaos. Okay, well, Waffles chased Bruce that is. And, now it was some weird game and her living room was the battleground.

Holly's eyes darted to her cat who ducked his head back under the branches before popping back up with an ornament in his mouth.

"Are you freaking kidding me?" She stared at Twitch in shock. "Is that what you were doing? Really, Twitch? Didn't we already talk about this?"

She was going to kill the cat, then Waffles, and while she was at it, Mildred and John too for good measure.

"Mom!" Jimmy ran up behind her freaking out as the chaos continued around them.

"Everything is fine, sweetie," she replied, staring at the vacated spot Twitch had just disappeared from. That cat was out to get her today and she was damn well sure of it. "Well, it'll be fine after I strangle the animals."

"Holy shit." Ben laughed as he grabbed the base of the tree putting it back in place. "And here I thought we were in the clear since you'd already cut yourself."

"That was Twitch's fault!" Holly stomped her foot.

"So this was Twitch's fault too?" Ben cocked his brow at her as his hand went to his stomach laughing.

"It was!" That's it. Screw it being Christmas. Everyone was on her list.

"Sure it was," Ben chuckled again picking up a few ornaments from the floor. "At least nothing's broken. We made sure to put away all the glass ones after the cat started taking them off the tree..." Ben trailed off as it suddenly dawned on him. He quickly glanced back to Holly who was cocking her brow at him. "Oh."

"Yeah, oh," she mocked, pointing at the tree. "He wanted another one to play with."

Just then, Twitch strolled out from under the tree carrying a red and green ball in his mouth as he headed toward Ben and Holly's room.

Instantly, Ben burst out into a deep laugh as everyone made their way into the living room to see what was going on.

"I'm so sorry," Emma apologized as Bruce ran to hide behind her legs. "I'm so *so* sorry. I don't know why he did that. He never even acts like a dog unless he's around you guys. On the one hand, that's a good thing but not if he does this. He's normally scared out of his mind at everything. I have no idea why he did that. I am *so* sorry."

The worried expression on Emma's face made Hollys' heart tighten.

"It's fine Emma. No harm, no foul." Ben sent her a soft smile. "We'll call it even since you made it so Holly wouldn't poison any of us."

That jerk. Holly angrily brought her attention back to Ben. "Who said I didn't?"

"She probably did," John replied. "We should have gone out to eat when we had the chance."

Holly narrowed her glare on John ready to attack. However, from the corner of her eye she saw Bruce still cowering behind Emma.

Oh, no. Her heart broke. *Maiming John can wait. This is far more important.*

Holly cautiously walked over to the big guy. It wasn't his fault. She knew that. "I'm not mad at you, Brucie... It's okay." Holly gently kissed his cowering head. "If I'm mad at anyone, it would be your ringleader. I'm sure this was his idea." Holly darted her eyes to Waffles who looked at her with his tongue hanging lopsided out of his mouth.

With a grunt, Holly decided it was best to ignore her asshole of a dog. As she shook her head, she turned back to Bruce, giving him another kiss on the head. "You're such a good, strong boy. Just try not to let the short one convert you to his evil ways, okay?" Holly gave him one more kiss before she lightly gave Emma's arm a squeeze, hopefully conveying to her it was all right.

Just then, Ripley trotted into the living room carrying the red ribbon and bow from last night making Holly's heart stop.

"What's that?" John asked, going over to Ripley.

"Mom, did Ripley find another present? I don't remember seeing any gifts with a bow that big on it?" Jimmy glanced over at her as panic raced through Holly.

"Ho-ly shit!" John bent over as he burst out laughing holding his stomach. "Was this the ribbon thing you were talking about earlier?"

"No!" Holly stormed over to her dog, snatching the ribbon and bow from her.

"Is that how you hurt your ankle?" Emma asked.

Holly wadded up the ribbon and bow as she quickly ran to the front door throwing them outside. Once they were gone, she slammed the door behind her. "I don't know what you're talking about. You saw nothing."

John turned to his best friend still gasping for air as he laughed. "Nice, dude. I have to admit I'm impressed."

"Stop talking!" Holly paced the room, sending a death glare to Ripley. *And here I thought you were my good child.*

"Not the show I was hoping for, but this will do." Mildred stepped further into the room, kicking a red ornament as she went. "Glad you took my advice on the inspiration part." She made eye contact with Ben. "You can thank me later."

A wicked smile appeared on Ben's face as he winked at the old woman. "I planned on sending you a box of chocolates the next time you were at the library."

"Make it an extra-large cheese pizza and I'll make sure to keep dropping a few gold nuggets into Holly's brain every once in a while." She winked at him.

"Deal."

For fuck's sake. Holly closed her eyes as she took a deep breath. *Why did I think hosting Christmas would be a good idea?* When Holly opened them she glared at the pain in her ass. "I'm sure your knitting club is going to eat this up, aren't they?"

"They're gonna love this." Mildred walked over to the coffee table to put her drink down. The moment she saw the stack of Christmas cards, she held one up as a mischievous grin appeared on the old coot's face. "Told ya you'd never get them out in time."

Holly growled as she picked up their tree topper, forcing herself to not toss it directly at Mildred's head.

Kill me now.

Mildred pumped her hands in the air as she did a victory dance around the room. "Detective Mildred strikes again!"

CHAPTER FIFTEEN

CHRISTMAS EVENING

Holly had done it. She'd actually done it. She'd pulled off a spectacular Christmas, and no one died.

At least as far as she knew.

As Mildred liked to point out as she walked out of their house an hour ago, she still needed to digest those potatoes. And if anything happened, she'd be calling Holly in the middle of the night. Even though Holly was pretty sure they were in the clear, just in case she planned on leaving her and Ben's phone in the living room.

You could never be too sure when Mildred was involved.

After dinner, everyone bundled up and went for a walk around the neighborhood to look at the Christmas lights. Which turned out incredible.

Holly wanted to pat herself on the back. Even though it was dark outside she'd only tripped twice. And each time Ben saved her from falling flat on her face.

Which was a record for her in the dark.

Then, of course, there was John the whole way around the block laughing at her, which of course included him bragging about his multiple race car wins. Although, Holly had a sneaking suspicion he was just trying to impress Emma.

John had even demanded to be the one to walk Bruce. Something about chivalry and all that.

And when John placed his arm around Emma's shoulder guiding her along the way, Holly noticed the faint hue of red on Emma's cheeks.

Maybe that was the real reason for her second *almost* face-plant. She was concentrating on them instead of where she was going.

At least she was now able to blame someone. And Holly figured that blaming John was just as satisfying as blaming Ben.

All in all, it really did turn out to be a perfect Christmas.

Holly: one million.

Everyone else: zero.

Wait, it's the holidays. Everyone else: one million, as well.

Holly placed Helen in her crib gently tucking her in. "Love you, baby girl. I hope your first Christmas was everything you could've ever wanted." Holly kissed her sleepy baby's head as Peanut gurgled one more time before closing her eyes. "Love you, sweet one."

"It was."

Holly turned to see Ben leaning against the door of Peanut's room. As she did a once-over of him, a soft smile appeared on her face.

"Come on, Holly." Ben held out his hand for her to take which she gladly did. "Let's go tuck our other tired boy into bed." While they walked hand-in-hand to Jimmy's room, the warmth of pure love and joy washed through Holly.

Nothing could get better than this. Once they got into Jimmy's room, they saw he was already in his pajamas and in his bed. His green race car tucked in right beside him.

"You can't sleep with that, kiddo."

"Why not?" he asked, eying Ben, nudging the toy closer to his side.

"It'll end up falling off the bed in the middle of the night, scare Waffles half to death and then, in turn, scare your mom, who would probably end up falling out of bed as well."

"Hey!" Holly punched his arm as she laughed. "Take that back."

As Ben took the toy from Jimmy placing it on the floor, he smirked at Holly.

"He's probably right, Mom."

Holly crossed her arms over her chest narrowing her eyes at both of them, as a smile spread across her face. "Well, he doesn't have to say it. And *you* don't have to agree."

Jimmy sent her a boyish grin. "Yeah, we do."

"Whatever," Holly mumbled, they were just lucky it was still Christmas.

Jimmy fidgeted on the bed, while he glanced up at them, biting his bottom lip. "Uh, Mom, Dad? Remember when we went to the mall and I sat on Santa's lap?"

"Yeah?"

The sweetest smile appeared on Jimmy's face as he spoke his next words. "I told Santa there wasn't anything I wanted for Christmas 'cause I already got what I wanted."

Holly cocked her head to the side as she watched her son. "Really?"

"I got it when you adopted me." His big eyes gazed up at her, revealing all the love he held for them.

"Oh, Jimmy..." Holly choked up as tears threatened to spill from her eyes.

"It's true, Mom. I love all this new stuff, don't get me wrong. But I would've been okay if Santa came and only brought stuff for Helen, Waffles, Ripley, and Twitch. I got the best present already and nothing can ever top that. I got you guys."

"Come here, Jimmy." Ben pulled him and Holly into his arms. The emotions in the room were almost too much for any of them to handle. "I love you, Jimmy."

"Love you too, Dad." He faced Holly. "You too, Mom. Even when you try to cook."

She leaned back cocking her head at her son. "Why do you have to ruin a perfect moment?"

"Every moment with you guys is perfect."

Holly's heart stopped as she watched her son give them a toothy grin that went from ear-to-ear.

Well, damn.

"This is the best Christmas I've ever had. Thank you."

What could you say to that? And here Holly was most of the season flipping out trying to give Jimmy the perfect holiday. Instead, he gave it to her. Between, Ben, Jimmy, her dad, and Peanut she had all she could ever want or need.

She really did luck out in this lifetime.

Hell, even her friends, actually, wait no, her *family* made everything an adventure for her. Even John and his ridiculous need to always have food in his mouth. She shook her head. At least Emma loved to cook.

As Holly watched her son, her heart filled with a love she never knew she could feel. "I love you, Jimmy."

"Love you too, Mom."

Jimmy scooted himself further into his bed. As Holly did her best to keep it together, her and Ben tucked Jimmy in, making sure to both give him a kiss on the head before walking out of his room gently closing the door behind them.

When they made it back into the living room, they saw Waffles on the floor happily chewing on the bone he'd gotten from Santa. Holly already knew Ripley and Twitch were fast asleep in the dog bed by Peanut's crib.

At least Waffles isn't trying to argue with anyone for once in his life. I should stuff his face with bones more often.

Holly plopped herself onto their couch kicking her feet up. Thank God, her ankle really was fine. It hadn't hurt once all day and she was sure as hell lucky she had Ben by her side. His medical expertise might be tailored to the four-legged kind, but it sure as hell helped her more times than she'd like to admit.

Holly let out a deep breath as she beamed at Ben. "This really did end up being a perfect Christmas, didn't it?"

"It certainly did. Even if you didn't get the Christmas cards out on time." He gave her a half smile. "Plus, you didn't break any bones in the process or strangle anyone. That makes it pretty damn perfect if you ask me."

Holly instantly tossed one of their throw pillows at his head. Which the jerk expertly avoided. "I'm never letting you live that down. I'm even gonna hang the photo I got for you in the office tomorrow."

Holly rolled her eyes. That's okay. She'd get him back sooner or later.

Out of nowhere, Twitch strolled into the living room and jumped onto the couch. "You nearly killed me today." Holly held up her bandaged finger waving it in his face.

Twitch ignored her as he bumped his head on her hand demanding attention. Holly sighed as she shook her head.

"You might be a pain in my ass but I still love you." She used her bandaged finger to bop him on the nose.

"That's what made it a perfect holiday."

Holly cocked her brow at Ben. "Twitch trying to kill me?"

"No." The corner of Ben's mouth quirked up as he reached over to scratch Twitch between the ears. "The memories. We'll never forget this holiday as long as we live."

"You're right." Holly glanced down at the cat purring away on her lap before turning her attention back to her husband. "Merry Christmas, Ben."

"Merry Christmas, Grace." Ben hauled Holly into his lap, making Twitch jump down as he kissed Holly on the lips.

When Waffles let out a whine Holly darted her eyes to him. "Geez, okay. Merry Christmas to you too, Lord Waffles." Holly rolled her eyes as his highness sent her a side-eye before plopping his head back down onto the floor.

"It's not like I hadn't wished you a Merry Christmas earlier?"

Waffles grunted.

"Can't you be more like your sister? She's in Peanut's room fast asleep *not* annoying the crap out of me."

Waffles picked his head up to scowl at her.

"One of these days, Waffles, I'm gonna—"

He stared her down as a deep noise came from his throat daring Holly to finish her sentence. She gave up shaking her head as she sighed. "Love you, Waffles."

At her words, his tongue fell out of the side of his mouth while he smiled at her.

"Oh, for the love of all things." Holly flicked her eyes to the ceiling before shifting back to Ben. "Why wasn't he on Santa's naughty list?"

"He'd find a way to murder us once he takes over the world," Ben answered, snuggling Holly into his lap deeper.

Waffles let out a small bark in agreement, causing Holly to shake her head as she growled at him in return.

"You might as well give up, Grace. He's never gonna change."

After a few moments, she gave up with a sigh. "You're right."

"I'm always right." Ben kissed her once more. "Merry Christmas, Holly."

"Merry Christmas, Ben."

"And, now it's time for *you* to unwrap *me*." A wicked smile appeared on Ben's face as he picked Holly up in his arms and carried her off to their bedroom only tripping over a runaway Waffles twice in the process.

EPILOGUE
NEW YEAR'S EVE

Holy crapolie!

It'd been a full week since Christmas, and somewhere along the way, Holly came up with the bright idea to invite everyone back over to ring in the New Year together.

Maybe she was a glutton for punishment? She still didn't know.

It only took her agreeing to not walk into the kitchen even once for everyone to be on board. She had to admit she was still a little pissed about it, though. She'd found a New Year's Eve party dip she wanted to make, but she decided to forgo it, wanting to spend the night with her family instead.

Plus, this made it so Emma brought most of the food. And Emma made *fantastic* food.

That bitch, Holly laughed to herself.

It didn't matter, though. Since Holly wasn't making the food it was really a win-win in her eyes.

Holly laughed again. Emma loving to cook was a good thing for John. Well, that was if Emma ever decided to pull her head out of her ass.

All in good time, though.

Holly knew sooner or later they would get together. They were meant to be. Just like her and Ben were.

"I'm extremely disappointed you don't have a life-size cake for someone to jump out of when the clock strikes midnight." Mildred eyed Holly crossing her arms over her sweater. The same sweater that had so many sparkles on it, every time Holly looked at her, she thought she'd go blind. "I was expecting some man chest today."

"Isn't it past your bedtime?" Holly placed her hand on her hip.

"Might be past *yours*, but it sure as hell ain't past mine. Isn't that right, Snookums?" Mildred glanced at her husband who nodded. "Sure thing, dear. Whatever you say."

Holly eyed him as she deadpanned, "You do know, you don't always have to agree with her, right?"

Mildred gave her husband a quick kiss on the cheek. "He learned a long time ago it was better this way."

"Don't we all," Ben agreed, as he slowly walked up to Holly.

"Watch it," Holly warned, before she gave him a quick kiss. "Did Jimmy go to sleep?"

"Yeah, he couldn't stay up no matter how hard he tried."

"Poor kid. There is always next year."

"Yeah." Ben smiled at her, kissing her once more.

"It's not midnight yet. Stop doing that." John gagged from the other side of the living room. "I wanna keep down my food."

"Not my problem," Holly remarked, as she yanked Ben into her arms to give him another big smacking kiss on the lips.

"Watch your hands there, son, that is my daughter you're manhandling," Henry chimed in seeing Ben's hand go to Holly's ass.

"She grabbed me, Henry. I have no control where my hands go after that."

"That's what I'm talking about." Mildred spun around to her husband. "This might be better than someone popping out of a cake after all."

"Do you ever stop talking?" Holly flicked her eyes up.

"No." Mildred shook her head.

"Figures." Just as Holly was about to say something else, Waffles waddled his butt into the room and plopped down in front of her. The moment he leaned over to lick Holly's right foot she snatched it back. "Stop doing that."

Ben chuckled as Waffles tried to do it again. "It's your fault you spilled the cheese dip on your foot to begin with, Grace."

"I cleaned it off." She narrowed her eyes at her dog.

Ben snickered. "Waffles doesn't think so."

"You're killing me here, Waffles." Holly pointed to John who was across the room. "Can't you go bug someone else?"

Waffles looked around the room before turning back to Holly. He then licked her foot one more time.

"Oh, for fuck's sake."

"Language, Pumpkin."

Holly growled snapping her attention to her dad. "Language my ass."

Henry cocked his brow at her as Ben burst out laughing.

"This is why I love coming over here," Mildred announced as she sat down with a bowl of popcorn in her lap and watched them.

"Me too." John grabbed a handful of popcorn from the bowl as he sat next to Mildred.

"Oh, no you don't." Mildred forcefully tugged the food away from John. "You've got your own work to deal with." She jutted her head toward Emma who was on her knees petting Bruce on the other side of the room.

"I'm working on it."

"Not fast enough," she replied. An evil smile emerged on Mildred's face. "Want me to help?"

John's whole face paled. "God no."

"You sure? I know people."

"And that's what scares me." John jumped up, the popcorn completely forgotten as he raced over to Emma's side shielding her from the old woman. When he glanced back toward Mildred, he sent her a glare. "You're not allowed to talk to her anymore."

"Young man, I can do whatever I damn well please. I didn't get this old not to have that right."

John pleadingly looked to Holly who shrugged. "This is her being a *mild* Mildred. I'd just deal with it before she gets a crazy idea in her whack-a-doo brain."

Mildred bolted to her feet. "I got it!" She pulled out her trusted notepad and started scribbling.

"We're all screwed."

Ben chuckled at Holly's annoyed expression. "Maybe she'll forget." He shrugged.

"I doubt it." Holly let out a sigh. "At least for once it's not us. Maybe Emma and John can be Mildred's new subjects at her knitting club."

"That's something you should've asked Santa for." Ben winked, giving Holly a quick peck on the lips.

"Maybe I did," Holly replied with a lopsided grin of her own.

"It's time!" Henry clapped his hands together.

"Everyone stop your yappin'. We got us a New Year to ring in!"

Ten, Nine, Eight, Seven, Six, Five, Four, Three, Two, One!

"Happy New Year!"

Ben pulled Holly into his arms as he kissed her like his life depended on it. "Here's to another great year," he whispered, pulling away from her lips for a second, before kissing her again.

Holly's entire face brightened as she lovingly gazed at her husband before going in for another kiss, herself. However, just as her lips were about to meet Ben's, she saw Emma had John pinned to the wall as they shared a kiss in the corner of the room.

"Whoa." Holly pointed at the two.

"Wonder how that's gonna turn out?" Ben remarked, with a chuckle.

A devious grin appeared on Holly's face. "Only one way to find out."

Before she could say anything more, Ben pulled her back into his embrace planting another kiss on her lips. "Best holiday season ever, Grace."

"It really was. Even if there were some stumbles along the way." Holly's smile went from ear-to-ear. "And, here is to many more holidays with you." Holly sealed her lips to Ben's once more.

Might as well start the New Year off right.

❄

John and Emma's story is up next in the Stumbling Through Life series. In the meantime, did the cat named Dog and his hunky firefighter owner intrigue you? If so, check out Teased by Fire. Or, was it the fashionista cat named Rupert? If so, check out Rupert, his owner Abbie and her archnemesis Hunter in Nothing But a Dare.

There is a sneak peek of Chapter one of Nothing But a Dare on the next page.

NOTHING BUT A DARE SNEAK PEEK
CHAPTER ONE

"I DARE YOU."

Hunter James raised his brow at ten-year-old Abbie Collins as she braced herself on the highest tree branch in their neighboring backyards. She quickly moved her eyes from him to reassess her surroundings. From where Abbie balanced, things weren't looking too good. How in the world had she gotten herself into this mess?

And again...

Her eyes moved back to the boy taunting her.

Oh yeah, how could she forget?

Hunter freaking James.

He's the reason she was now in a tree.

Since Hunter moved in next door with his dad and step-mom, he was constantly causing trouble. And somehow, Abbie was always involved.

She closed her eyes as she held onto the tree trunk tightly.

The day Hunter and his family moved in, Abbie and her mother, Kathleen, brought them over fresh baked cookies. That was the nice thing to do, after all. The neighborly thing.

Plus, Abbie had been particularly proud of this batch since she spent hours decorating each one with the word 'welcome'.

Abbie, along with her mother, had considered herself the welcoming committee of the neighborhood.

Ehh, what could she say? She got her nurturing side from her mom. Plus, Abbie absolutely adored making new friends. You could *never* have too many if you asked her.

The more, the merrier.

Maybe it was because Abbie didn't have any brothers or sisters, or maybe it was her need for everyone to feel like they belonged.

After her father abandoned her and her mom right after Abbie was born there was always something lacking. That could've been the reason why her mother always made it a point to welcome anyone that moved in with wide open arms and a plate full of cookies. She needed them to feel wanted since they'd never felt that.

Well, that plate full of cookies was two years ago and every day since meeting Hunter James, Abbie regretted every freaking second of it.

"Are you gonna do it or what?" Hunter taunted from below. "You better hurry, I don't know if that branch will hold you much longer?"

Jerk. Abbie's eyes narrowed at him as she held onto the tree trunk a little tighter. If she could go back in time, she would have added salt to the cookies, or better yet, maybe some arsenic.

"Stop being a baby, Collins."

"I'm not being a baby!" Abbie felt the branch bend under her weight.

Quickly, she closed her eyes as her heart started to pound against her chest. Okay, so she knew she was only about six feet off the ground, and the likelihood of her causing severe damage was slim to none; however, the more she looked at the annoying boy below her, the farther away he seemed.

Abbie took a deep breath before she opened her eyes and looked back at Hunter.

That's when she noticed it.

Hunter was staring at her with that stupid smug smirk on his face. The same one he always got when he thought he'd won.

A growl erupted from deep inside her. *Not today!*

If Abbie were on the ground and *not* a million feet in the air, she'd march right up to him and smack that dang smirk right off his stupid face.

Stupid Hunter.

Stupid tree.

Stupid dare!

For two years now, Hunter James had made her life a living hell.

If he wasn't constantly picking on her, he was daring her to do something she didn't want to do.

And *that* was the exact reason she was up in a tree right now.

"You're too scared, Abbie." Hunter laughed as he crossed his arms over his chest.

"Am not. I just think it's dumb to jump out of a tree unless there is a logical reason to do so."

"Why do you always do that?" He glared at her.

"Do what?"

"Say shit to make you sound all smart and stuff."

"I am smart, unlike you dumb-dumb."

Hunter's eyes narrowed before his lips formed into that smirk. *"I dare you."*

A Collins never surrendered.

A Collins never backed down.

A Collins never turned down a dare.

At least that's what her mother would say. Okay, not so much the dare part, but the never backing down part. Collins' were strong, and no matter what was thrown at them, they always ended up on top.

No one will ever knock us down.

Not her deadbeat father, and certainly not Hunter James.

And that left Abbie here.

About to jump to her death.

She rolled her eyes at herself. *Maybe death was a little dramatic.* She took another deep breath before looking at the ground. Her breath caught in her throat as Hunter suddenly seemed very far away. *Actually, death could be a possibility.*

"You scared?" Hunter shouted.

"Not as scared as you were when I dared you to jump off the roof into the pool," she snapped.

"I did it, didn't I?"

"Only after I called you a chicken," she yelled back. Why couldn't she have just walked away? Any other normal human being would have, but no. Abbie was now two years deep in some messed up back and forth dare-off.

"And that's what you're being right now. Abbie the chicken!" The corner of his mouth turned up into that stupid smirk again. "That's your new name."

"When I get down there, I'm gonna hit you!"

"You'd have to catch me first."

Abbie's eyes narrowed in on her target. She hated him. With every ounce of her being, she hated Hunter James.

Screw it.

She jumped.

Thankfully something broke her fall.

That something being Hunter James.

"What the hell?" Hunter cried. "You weren't supposed to jump on me, Collins."

"You never specified what I had to do in the dare. If you wanted to make sure I *didn't* jump on you, then you needed to disclose those terms upfront." She huffed as she righted herself making it so she sat on Hunter's chest. She then pushed her chestnut hair out of her face. "It's not my fault your dumb brain forgot that part."

"Who talks like that?" He squirmed trying to get her off. "Has anyone ever told you, you're annoying?"

"Yes, you. Every day."

"You're ten. You're not some genius." Hunter pushed her off him, causing her to land on her butt in the dirt.

From where she landed, Abbie watched as he fixed his clothes before pushing his black hair out of his face, giving her the view of his hunter green eyes that matched his name. "Excuse you, I turn eleven in two days." Abbie stuck her tongue out at him as she jumped to her feet.

"Oh, that reminds me..." Hunter pulled a tiny box out of his pocket. "This is for you."

Abbie took a step back caught entirely off-guard. Then out of nowhere, her heart did this weird flip thing she couldn't explain.

As she stared at him, with her mouth open in disbelief. She quickly tried to scan her body. She was ten, so there was no way she was having a heart attack. Right? When Hunter pushed the box closer to her, her heart did it again.

What the hell? Am I dying? Oh, God, the jump really did kill me. And, of course, this is now my hell. A hell where Hunter James existed.

"Take the box, Abbie," Hunter scoffed annoyed.

Had he really gotten her a birthday gift? She looked at the box and then back to his face. He *seemed* sincere. But then again, this was Hunter after all.

Abbie bit her bottom lip as she took the box. *Maybe this is the end of the feud...or, you know, maybe it was a bomb.* There was a fifty-fifty shot of either one.

Screw it. That was Abbie's motto when it came to Hunter.

She opened the box.

"Eww!" Before Abbie knew what was happening, grasshoppers started jumping out causing her to drop the box.

"Happy Birthday!" Hunter laughed as Abbie danced around trying to get the creatures off. "You're a jerk, Hunter."

"No, I'm not." He took a step closer to her plucking one of the grasshoppers off her shoulder. "I dare you to eat it."

"No way!" Abbie shook her head stepping back from him.

"You scared, little girl?" He pushed the grasshopper closer to her face.

"No, I'm not scared."

"Abbie the chicken. I knew the name would fit."

Screw it!

Abbie snatched the grasshopper from Hunter's fingers before shoving the thing into her mouth causing Hunter's eyes to widen for a split second before his amusement overtook him. "Holy crap. I can't believe you did it."

"Of course, I did," she said disgusted with herself. "I'm *not* a chicken."

"Abbie Babbie, the one with too much flabby," Hunter laughed.

"That's it." Abbie launched herself at Hunter tackling him to the ground. "What's your problem?"

"I don't have a problem. *You* have a problem." He fought from under her.

"Oh, that's really mature." Abbie kept him pinned to the ground. She'd learned a few things from their past wrestling matches. Like how locking her knees around his chest would prevent him from moving for at least a few seconds.

"I *am* a mature person. I'm almost thirteen. That makes me almost a teenager." Hunter looked at her. The moment her eyes locked with his green ones, that strange feeling in her heart came back. Maybe she *was* having a heart attack.

"You're a jerk."

"You always say that."

"That's 'cause it's true."

Hunter grunted before pushing Abbie off him effectively flipping her onto the ground. "Whatever. Why don't you run on home and stick your head in one of those stupid books you always have with you?"

"How is that an insult?" Abbie crossed her arms over her chest. "You make it seem like reading is a *bad* thing. Maybe if you picked up a book every once in a while, you'd actually learn something."

"Oh, like the books *you* read teach you anything?" He cocked his brow.

"Duhh. They teach me all kinds of stuff." Abbie walked to her bag and threw one of her books at him. "I dare you."

Hunter caught it with ease. "You dare me to what?"

"Read a book. Learn something. Stop being such an ass-hat."

Ignoring her new insult, Hunter cocked his head to the side. "You want me to read *Treasure Island?* This isn't English class, Collins."

"What are you scared you might actually learn something?"

Abbie knew she had him. Hunter *never* turned down a dare from her. Just like she never turned down a dare from him. "I *dare* you to read that whole book, Hunter."

His eyes shot to hers as they narrowed. "Fine." He placed the book under his arm as he turned away from her. After walking a few steps, he looked over his shoulder. "A dare's a dare. Just remember this isn't over."

Would it ever be?

❄

Continue Abbie and Hunter's story in Nothing But a Dare.

ALSO BY MOLLY O'HARE

Stumbling Through Life Series

Stumbling Into Him

Stumbling Into Forever

Stumbling Into the Holidays

John & Emma's story – *Coming soon*

Teased by Love Series

Teased by Fire

Teased by Tinsel

Lucas & Miranda's story – Coming soon

Hollywood Hopeful Series

Hollywood Dreams

Risking It All (Danny and Lexi's Story) – *Coming soon*

Standalone Novels

Nothing But a Dare

Learning Curves

Stay Connected

Sign up for my newsletter or check out my website.

If you just want to hang out, come join my reader group: Molly's
Badass Babes.

ABOUT THE AUTHOR

Molly O'Hare is a USA Today Bestselling author of plus size romance books.

She grew up with severe dyslexia and neurodivergence, trust her, spelling is not her strong suit. Over the years, she's become a huge advocate of "just because you learn something a little differently than others does not make you less in any way." She also advocates for body positivity in all shapes and sizes. And, to say Molly is obsessed with all things animals is probably an understatement.

When she was younger, she had a wicked case of insomnia most nights, and to help herself fall asleep, she would create stories in her head, always picking up where she left off the night before. Then, one morning she figured if she got endless enjoyment out of her imagination, others might as well. And thus started her career as an author.

And as she always likes to say, never forget how absolutely unique and beautiful you are. The world is better because you are here.

I think I will bestow upon you some fun facts about me.

Fun Facts for Stumbling Into the Holidays:

My husband fell through our ceiling this year. That's where the scene came from. He was fine. Just his ego was hurt. There are pictures of this in my reader group if you want a good laugh.

My Corgi's Frank and Lillian are more like Lord Waffles than you think.

I love Sushi.

I strive to be Mildred when I'm older.

I am obsessed with candles. Like really obsessed. It's almost scary, but shh, that will be our secret.

I was pushed out of the bed this morning by Frank, and my husband still says it was me and not the dog. That jerk. :)

Stay Connected

Made in the USA
Monee, IL
15 September 2022